Dear Brio Girl,

Some things change: history, fashion, the weather. And some things you change: your socks (hopefully), your mind, your classes. But some things never change . . . like the fact that God is absolutely crazy about you . . . and the fact that He wants your fulfillment even more than you do!

But learning to trust Him with the changes that happen in your life isn't always easy. At least it's not for Becca. Can you identify? If so, you've found a lifetime friend. Get to know her through this book. I think you'll be glad you did!

Your Friend,

Susie Shellenberger, BRIO Editor
www.briomag.com

Brio Girls

● ● ●

Stuck in the Sky
by Lissa Halls Johnson

Fast Forward to Normal
by Jane Vogel

Fast Forward to Normal

Created by

LISSA HALLS JOHNSON

WRITTEN BY JANE VOGEL

BETHANYHOUSE
MINNEAPOLIS, MINNESOTA

Fast Forward to Normal

Cover design by Lookout Design Group, Inc.

A Focus on the Family book.
Published by Bethany House Publishers
A Ministry of Bethany Fellowship International
11400 Hampshire Avenue South
Bloomington, Minnesota 55438
www.bethanyhouse.com

Printed in the United States of America by
Bethany Press International, Bloomington, Minnesota 55438

Library of Congress Cataloging-in-Publication Data

Vogel, Jane.
Fast forward to normal / by Jane Vogel.
p. cm. — (Brio girls)
Summary: High-school junior Becca finds herself resentful when her parents discuss adopting Alvaro, the ill Guatemalan boy staying with them temporarily.
ISBN 1-56179-952-1
[1. Adoption—Fiction. 2. Schools—Fiction. 3. Christianlife—Fiction.]
I. Title. II. Series.
PZ7.V8672 Fas 2001
[Fic]—dc21

2001002628

To Steve, Marie, and Peter,
who made Becca and Alvaro part of the family.

Special thanks to the girls at Wheaton CRC, especially

- *Stephanie* for ongoing input via e-mail at all hours of the day and night;
- *Aubrey* for her role as Spanish/English dictionary;
- *Amie, Alli,* and *Lauren* for reviewing the manuscript;

and to my own girlfriends—
we're never too old to need each other!

JANE VOGEL has been active in youth ministry for nearly twenty years as a writer and youth worker. She is the author of several books and a contributor to several study Bibles. Jane received her MCE from Calvin Theological Seminary.

chapter 1

JOURNAL

THURSDAY, OCTOBER 4

T minus 21 days and counting. Only three more weeks of Alvaro. If life came with a remote control, I'd have my thumb on the fast-forward button right now.

Everybody thinks our family is wonderful for taking Alvaro in after his surgery. I thought so too—at first. Now I'm ready for him to go home so we can get on with our lives.

I'm sick of tiptoeing around after eight p.m. so Alvaro can get to sleep. Of waking up to his nightmare screams. Of doing extra chores so Mom has time to drive him all the way to the Denver hospital and back twice a week. I'm even sick of the way that nasty medicated salve smells!

But how can I tell anyone that I'm fed up with a poor, sick little boy? I'd sound like a monster. Sometimes I feel like one.

21 more days.

The 2:30 bell rang and Becca McKinnon jerked her attention back to algebra class. Oops. She was supposed to be getting a head start on the day's assignment, and instead she'd been scribbling down her thoughts. Oh, well. She'd do the homework tonight. She tore the journaled page out of her spiral notebook and crammed it into the pocket of her cargo shorts. Grabbing her books, she joined the group of laughing and talking students already pressing through the doorway and into the hall.

"Hey, Becca!"

Becca grinned and waved as she spotted Katie Spencer weaving her way toward her through the crowded hall.

"How come you're not on the volleyball team this year?" Katie asked. "We could use your hustle!"

"Yeah, I was going to be your power spiker this year," Becca quipped, pulling herself up to her full 5'7".

"Don't sell yourself *short*, girl," Katie said, echoing their coach's refrain from the previous year. "You've got more on the ball than some of those 5'10" players. So what gives? I never thought I'd see you giving up sports."

"No way! I'm not giving up sports. I'd rather die!" Becca said. "I'm just taking the fall season off—I'll definitely be playing basketball this winter. But I can't fit volleyball in with paragliding. The good weather isn't going to hold out much longer. I don't want to spend every afternoon at practice when I could be gliding."

Katie rolled her eyes. "Think of me sweating on the court while you're gliding today, will you?"

"Actually, today I can't—" But Katie had spotted a couple of other volleyball players and dashed off to join them before Becca could finish. Becca stood still for a second watching them go. Katie was one of the most popular girls in the junior class. Becca didn't like to think that popularity was all that important to her, but she had the sudden, painful feeling of being left out. *Maybe it was a mistake to give up volleyball*, she thought.

Shaking her head as if she could throw off any regrets, Becca turned to the wall of lockers, counted five lockers from the classroom door, and set to work on the lock.

"Let's see—21 right, 8 left, 52 right." She frowned as she murmured her combination under her breath. "Or is it 21 *left?*" She gave the lock a good yank. It didn't open. She yanked again, smacking the locker for good measure. Still no success. Frustrated, she started spinning the dial again.

"Trying to break into my locker, McKinnon?"

Becca jumped and looked up. Nate Visser towered over her, a mock frown on his face while his blue eyes sparkled mischievously.

"Third time this month," Nate teased. "Am I really supposed to believe you still think this is your locker?" He grinned. "What is it you find so intriguing about me that you have to pull this mistaken-locker-identity stunt?"

"Keep dreaming!" Becca retorted, straightening up to face Nate. She noticed that, even standing her tallest, she had to tilt her head up to look him in the eye. "A simple miscalculation, that's all. I was talking to Katie. She distracted me."

Nate shook his head. "Honestly, Becca," he said, "how can a girl as coordinated as you be so directionally challenged? You do know your left from your right, don't you?"

"Sure," Becca answered, tucking her books under her arm and holding her hands in front of her. "My left hand is the one that looks like an L."

Nate groaned as he saw Becca's left hand, palm down, and her right hand, palm up, both forming the letter L.

"Very funny." He put his hands on her shoulders and marched her to the algebra classroom. "Stand here," he said, backing into the doorway with Becca in front of him so that they both faced into the hall. Becca felt a little shiver run up her spine, as if Nate's hands had started an electrical current running through her. *Does Nate feel it too?* she wondered. *Do I want him to?*

Still grasping her shoulders, Nate turned Becca to the left and said, "Look—to the left you're heading toward the cafeteria. *My* locker is five lockers *left* of your algebra class going *toward* the cafeteria." He pivoted Becca to the right. "Your locker is five lockers to the *right* of your algebra class, *toward* the gym. It's easy, Becca. Your locker, like you, is tied to the gym."

Nate let go of Becca's shoulders and looked speculatively at her. "You know, when you first started showing up at my locker this year, I thought maybe you were stalking me." Becca raised her eyebrows and waited for him to continue. "But I asked Tyler and he assured me it was just your problem with directions and not my personal magnetism." As Becca began to laugh, Nate hastily continued, "So, what it is about Tyler, anyway, that he gets to hang out with all you girls? What's his secret attraction?"

"Not what you're thinking," Becca told him. "I mean, I know a lot of girls think Tyler's hot, but I never see him that way. He's just Tyler." Somehow it seemed important to make sure Nate understood that she wasn't attracted to Tyler that way. Becca shrugged. "I guess it's because we've been friends practically forever."

She thought about this for a second. "Since fourth grade, anyway," she amended. "We started this club, Tyler and Jacie and Solana and me. Later when we got into reading *Brio* magazine we sometimes called each other *Brio* sisses like the editor, Susie Shellenberger, does."

Nate raised one eyebrow. "And Tyler?"

Becca laughed. "Tyler's our honorary *Brio* brother—partly because he's always been our best friend and partly because his mom is on staff at *Brio*." Becca stopped. "Am I rambling? You already know about *Brio*, I guess."

Nate nodded. "Yeah. It's girl stuff. I've been to a couple of photo shoots." Tyler's mom sometimes used Tyler and his friends for models in the magazine.

"Anyway, the magazine got us talking about God and faith and how we should live our lives. I guess that's part of what keeps us so close," Becca concluded.

"So you see Tyler like a brother." Nate seemed to want to be sure about this point.

"Definitely," Becca confirmed. "One happy family—that's what we are."

"Sometimes things change," prodded Nate.

"I know," Becca agreed, thinking of Katie and the volleyball team. Then she smiled confidently. "But not our little group of friends!"

● ● ●

Becca retrieved her homework, slung her backpack over one shoulder, and headed out across the quad to find the rest of her friends. It was a comfortable habit they'd gotten into, meeting after school to see what everybody else was doing with the rest of the day.

Solana and Tyler were already in the quad, sitting on the table under "their" tree. In front of them, Jacie was bobbing from one foot to the other as if she were dancing to some upbeat music only she could hear, waving her hands and talking a mile a minute, her face lit up with excitement.

"Becca!" Jacie exclaimed as soon as she saw her. "Guess what? You'll never believe it! The junior class officers asked me to design the window for homecoming!"

"That's awesome, Jacie! Of course I believe it. Everybody knows you're the best artist in the school. No—what am I saying? Your painting of Damien took grand prize in the Copper Ridge art show—you're the best artist in the city!"

Jacie beamed with undisguised pleasure at her friends. As Becca exchanged an affectionate "isn't she cute when she's excited?" look with Solana and Tyler, she saw that they weren't the only ones at the table. Perched primly on the bench behind the table, half hidden by Solana and Tyler, who were lounging on top of the table, sat Hannah Connor. *With that gorgeous blond hair and that perfect figure, she'd be a knockout*, Becca thought, *if only she'd lose the bun and dress a little less like somebody's librarian aunt.* She threw a suspicious glance at Tyler. Those tall, Nordic types were his weakness.

"Jacie, I'm happy that you've received such an honor," Hannah said. "But I don't really know what you're talking about, being a homeschooled girl and all. You are to design which window? Where?"

Becca caught Solana's eye. Hannah was new to Stony Brook High this year. Once Jacie introduced Hannah to the group, she'd just sort of glommed onto them. Sometimes Becca thought Hannah wasn't even trying to fit in anywhere else. Every chance Hannah got, she reminded people that she had been homeschooled. *Which is fine*, Becca thought, *but we've heard all about it. It's time to move on.*

Tyler didn't seem to mind, though. He was leaning over Hannah eagerly. "See, every year the downtown businesses let the high schools paint their windows for homecoming. Of course, every class wants to paint the best window. Last year our class painted our school mascot, the Studs—I mean, the Stallions," he hastily revised at Hannah's sharp intake of breath. "Usually they try to do something with the homecoming theme, too."

"That's what's so great about getting to do the design," Jacie cut in. "This year's theme is 'Celebrate the Good Times,' right? Well, you know how many keggers there are—"

"Keggers are the kids who drink," Tyler helpfully explained to Hannah.

"And you know what kinds of things other kids do with a theme like 'Good Times,'" Jacie continued. "So I thought it would be a great chance for me to paint a window that shows different kinds of good times. You know, let people see that not all teenagers are into partying and stuff."

"Oh, yeah, girl," Solana joined in. "You could even work the Stallions into that. Horseback riding as good times. We can go out to my uncle's ranch and use his horses as models." She grinned slyly and shot Jacie a sideways glance. "I'll tell my uncle you need *hours* of watching me gallop for your sketches. He'll be so proud to think of me as a model of *Latina* womanhood that he'll let me ride as much as I want!"

"Hey, here's an idea, Jacie," Tyler interjected. "You could do a sort of collage—"

"Montage," Jacie murmured automatically.

"—of different interests and hobbies," Tyler went on. "Stuff people do for good times. Like Solana and her horseback riding. Becca going climbing or gliding or something. And I could pose with my guitar."

There was a second's silence as Becca, Jacie, and Solana looked at one another, then they all began talking at once, each on a different subject, none of them having to do with music. Tyler, looking a little confused, finally shrugged, and turned to ask Hannah what she liked to do for fun.

Becca put her arm around Jacie and gave her a squeeze. "Whatever ideas you come up with, I know they'll be really creative. And I think it's so cool to use the window to make a statement about positive stuff." She looked at Jacie head on. "You know, Jacie, that's a really great way to express your faith."

Jacie smiled a little shyly. "Thanks, Becca. I want to get better at doing that. I wish I were as comfortable expressing it in words as you are."

"Hey, a picture paints a thousand words, right?" Becca added seriously, "Jacie, just be you. And be real. That's all it takes."

"When God closes a door, he always opens a window," Hannah's voice cut across their conversation, and Becca scrunched her eyes shut for a second in silent frustration. She hated to hear Christians spouting clichés—it sounded so phony.

"Or in this case," Hannah continued, "God uses a window to open a door." She turned from Tyler to address Jacie. "I think it's wonderful to have a Christian in charge of the window so we can denounce the drugs, sex, and rock 'n' roll that pass for good times in this secular high school."

"Uh-oh," Becca murmured under her breath, and looked at Solana.

"Well, that's my cue to get off my secular butt and go," Solana said cheerfully. "I don't actually have any drugs or sex planned for the afternoon, but mmm-mmm, that rock 'n' roll is calling my name." She cocked an eyebrow at Hannah, gave a little shimmy, and sauntered out of the quad.

"Wait up, Solana!" Becca called. "I'll walk you to the parking lot." She ran to catch up with Solana as the others followed more slowly.

"Sex, drugs, and rock 'n' roll!" Solana fumed.

"I know," Becca hissed. *And when did God appoint Hannah the judge of this "secular high school"? She hasn't even been here two months! Good thing Solana knows that not all Christians are like that.* Becca took a couple of deep breaths to try to calm down. She knew she wasn't being fair to Hannah. They had all gone to the *Brio* Faith Fest conference last month and Hannah was really good with the adults she talked to. Maybe she just had trouble getting along with other teenagers.

"Hannah," Becca said, slowing down to let the others catch up, "I don't believe in drugs or premarital sex, either." She decided not to say anything about rock music. "I know you've had some great experiences sharing your faith, but I don't think 'denouncing' people is going to be a successful way to share your faith here at school."

"God doesn't call us to be successful," Hannah replied complacently, "just faithful."

"Maybe," Becca agreed, "but there's nothing unfaithful about wanting to make your faith attractive." *More attractive even than Tyler seems to find you, even if you do look like a Barbie doll—with a bad wardrobe*, she added silently.

"Well . . . but I think you're right, Hannah," Jacie said hesitantly. "Maybe not about denouncing, exactly, but about standing up for what you believe." She threw an apologetic glance at Becca, then turned back to Hannah. "I'd like to hear more about your ideas."

She doesn't mean it, Becca thought. *She's only trying to smooth things over. And I wish she wouldn't. Hannah will just keep spouting her pat answers.*

"How about we all go to Copperchino for coffee?" Tyler suggested. "We can talk there."

"Can't," said Becca shortly, as they reached the bike rack at the edge of the parking lot. "Today's my mom's staff meeting at the community center and I promised I'd be home to watch Alvaro."

Hannah nodded approvingly. "Jacie told me about the wonderful things your family is doing for that little alien boy. Your family must be very special." She smiled—rather condescendingly, Becca felt.

"Don't call him an alien," Becca replied in exasperation. She didn't need anybody else telling her how special her family was. Anyway, since when had Jacie been discussing Becca's family with

Hannah? "You make him sound like Jar-Jar Binks. He's from Guatemala, not some galaxy far, far away."

Hannah quickly put her hand to her mouth. "Oh, I didn't mean that kind of alien," she explained. "I meant like, resident alien or illegal alien, you know? Not that your little boy is illegal . . ." Hannah stammered to a halt, seeming to realize that she was making things worse.

"Maybe Hannah thinks Hispanics *belong* in a galaxy far, far away," Solana said with a Mexican accent so exaggerated that even her own mother, who spoke Spanish at home, wouldn't recognize it. Turning to Hannah, she bowed. "*Hola, senorita!* Take me to your leader for American drugs, sex, and rock 'n' roll."

Becca erupted in a snort of laughter. Solana always could joke her out of a bad mood. Tyler frowned and said, "Lighten up, Solana!" Becca flashed Solana a quick thumbs-up.

She leaned closer to Solana, trying to choke back her laughter. "What do you think will happen when Hannah discovers that Tyler wants to be in a rock band?" she whispered to Solana. She glanced at the others to make sure they couldn't hear. No problem. Tyler had launched into some long story in an apparent effort to get Hannah's mind off her embarrassment.

"Worse—what if he finally *does* get a band together and she hears him sing?" Solana hissed back. "Poor Tyler! Any girl he tries to serenade had better be tone-deaf." Becca reached inside the neck of her T-shirt and pulled out the three chains that hung inside her shirt. Slipping the chain holding a bike key over her head, she bent over the bike rack, quickly unfastened the lock—no combination to slow her down—and freed her mountain bike from the rack. A lot of the upperclassmen drove to school, but Becca's brother, Matt, had taken the family's third car to college when he'd left this fall, and Becca's parents had been so busy with Alvaro's foster care that they hadn't gotten around to buying a beater for Becca to drive. Not that she minded. She'd rather bike than drive any day—well, any day that it wasn't raining. Or sleeting, or . . . Come to think of it, given the unpredictability of Colorado weather, she hoped her parents would buy another car in the next month or so.

"Yo—Tyler!" a deep voice called, and Becca straightened up quickly. "So," Nate said, "have you guys made plans for homecoming yet? I thought maybe a bunch of us could go together." He kept his eyes steadily on Tyler. "You know, Richard, J.P., me, and—" his eyes flicked toward Becca, then back to Tyler "—all you guys. Maybe Damien?" he said, now looking at Jacie. He shifted from one foot to the other. "Unless you already have plans?"

"Me, I already have a date," Solana said with a satisfied smile.

"Let me guess," teased Tyler. "Dennis Sanchez asked you."

Solana tossed her head. "Dennis asked me to homecoming the first week of school. And the second. But I'm going with Derek Harris." Giving Becca a quick, barely perceptible wink, she added, "There's no reason the rest of you shouldn't go together, though."

"Sounds good to me," Tyler agreed, while Becca and Jacie nodded their heads. "We'll set up the details later. Hey, Jacie, do you have your car here today? My car's in the shop and I could use a ride—how about you, Hannah?"

Becca turned back to her bike. Sliding the scrunchie out of her hair, she shook out the ponytail that never fit quite right under her helmet. Her wavy brown hair fell past her shoulders.

"I like your hair like that!" Nate put out a hand as if to touch it, then abruptly changed direction and scratched the back of his neck instead. "I don't think I've ever seen you wear it down before."

"Oh, I usually pull it back to keep it out of the way," Becca replied. *But maybe I should wear it loose more often,* she thought, looking at Hannah's severe bun.

Hannah was deep in conversation with Tyler and Jacie, and Becca thought she looked half-defiant, half—what? Pleading? Regretful? Becca couldn't tell. Hannah looked uncertain, which seemed strange since she always made her pronouncements as if they came straight from God.

Tyler turned back to Nate and Becca. "Homecoming isn't going to work out for Hannah."

"My heart is breaking," Becca said in an undertone to Solana.

"So how about we all get together at your house instead, Becca?" Tyler suggested. "You know, hang out in your family room and play air hockey and stuff."

"Right," said Becca. "Like we'd want to play air hockey instead of going to the homecoming dance."

Jacie spoke. "It would be so fun to go to homecoming together. But we can't leave Hannah out. Her parents aren't comfortable with her going to events like that," she explained. "But they'd let her get together with friends at somebody's house." She shifted her gaze to Nate. "You know we always have a good time when we go to Becca's," she urged. "You and Richard and J.P. could come, too."

Becca felt as if she'd walked into some weird sitcom where she didn't know her lines. How had a group date to homecoming suddenly morphed into sitting around at her house? She was about to tell Nate she'd like to go to homecoming with him even if the rest of the group didn't go, then stopped. *He didn't actually ask* me, she reminded herself. *He asked the group.*

Tyler was acting as if everything was settled, but Nate looked uncomfortable. "No offense, Becca," he said. "Hanging out at your house is great. But some other time, maybe. I really don't want to skip homecoming." With a puzzled frown and a half-apologetic wave, he turned and loped across the parking lot.

"Thanks a lot, guys," Becca hissed furiously. "Did you hear me invite you to my house for homecoming?"

"Sorry, Becca," Tyler began. "But we always go to your house. You've never minded before."

"We go to my house on *ordinary* weekends," Becca corrected. "Not during homecoming."

"Well, maybe this year things need to be different. Now that Hannah's part of the group . . ." Tyler left the sentence unfinished.

Becca opened her mouth, then shut it again quickly. "Listen, I've got to go. My mom will kill me if I'm late," she finally said, and pulled her bike from the rack.

Skirting the parking lot, she turned onto Stony Brook Road and sped down the steep hill in front of the school, her thoughts racing as fast as her bicycle. Since when was Hannah part of their group? Sure, she'd been hanging around a lot, but wasn't that only because Jacie had introduced her the first day of school and she didn't know anyone else? Tyler was clearly attracted to Hannah—but he ought to know *that* would never work in a group where the rest of them were like brother and sisters. They were the group that was never supposed to change.

At the first intersection Becca rounded the corner and leaned into the next hill to begin the ascent. *What's the matter with me?* she asked herself. *I'm the one who's always wanting to meet new people and try new things. Why do I have a problem with Hannah?* She crouched lower over her handlebars and pedaled harder, as if speed would help her think. *Is it because she messed up my chance to go out with Nate? I don't want to be one of those girls who dumps her friends for some guy.* Shaking her head slightly, Becca answered her own question. *No, it's more than that. It's the way Hannah is messing with our tight group of friends. She's got Tyler all goofy about her. She butted into Jacie's business with the art show last month. And she has no idea how to be friends with a non-Christian like Solana.*

With each pump of the pedals Becca pushed out her frustration. Pump. *We used to have so much fun together. Now Hannah is spoiling everything.* Pump, pump. *I don't even really like Hannah. We don't have anything in common—except being Christians. Does being a Christian mean I have to be friends with everybody?* Pump, pump. She picked up speed as she crested the hill and started down the other side.

God, I'm confused. Shouldn't doing what's right make me glad, not frustrated? Unconsciously Becca squeezed her eyes shut as she concentrated on her prayer. *I'm not exactly expecting any big reward for helping out with Alvaro and being friendly to Hannah, but—*

Ooomph! With a lurch, Becca felt her bike come to an abrupt stop, and she sailed over the handlebars.

chapter 2

Becca sat up and gingerly flexed her arms and legs. Nothing broken. Her right leg was a little scraped, and so were her palms—thank goodness her subconscious self had enough sense to fling out her hands to break her fall. If only her conscious self were as sensible.

What a dope, she chided herself. *Closing your eyes while you're biking!* She looked around for her bike. It lay on the side of the road just past a fist-sized rock. *I must have hit the rock while I was praying*, she realized. Her bike was fine—maybe a scrape or two in the paint, but Becca had put so many nicks in the finish while biking on mountain trails that she couldn't really tell if the scrapes she saw now were new or old.

"Is this Your idea of a joke, God?" she said out loud. "I'm asking for blessings and You give me a bump on the head? Well,

You've got my attention, but I'll tell You one thing—I'm praying with my eyes open from now on." She straddled her bike and began coasting down the hill. "But thank You for keeping me and my bike from getting bashed up," she added. At the bottom of the hill she pedaled furiously until she reached home.

Becca raced up the driveway, threw her bike in the grass, and sprinted to the house, unstrapping her helmet as she ran.

"Sorry I'm late, Mom!" she yelled as she pulled open the front door.

Her mom came out of the kitchen, checking her wristwatch. "Not too late," she said, kissing Becca on the forehead. "I can still make my meeting on time. What happened to you?" she said, noticing Becca's scrapes.

"I was praying and I went airborne," Becca told her. "It's kind of a long story."

"It must have been some prayer," her mom said, calmly examining Becca's hands and leg. "I don't think there's enough blood here to make me miss my meeting. Just wash it off and you should be fine."

Becca nodded. "Hi, Alvaro," she said as a thin little figure appeared in the kitchen doorway, clutching a battered Cheerios box to his chest. With his other hand he reached out to clutch Mrs. McKinnon's skirt.

"I'm going to work, Alvaro." Becca's mom gently pried Alvaro's fingers loose. "Becca will get you a snack, okay?" She turned to Becca. "That reminds me: Will you make supper tonight? Dad should be home around six."

"Mom! It's Kassy's turn to make supper. I cooked last time."

"I hardly think making macaroni and cheese from a box counts as cooking," her mother observed dryly.

"Well, we were out of frozen pizza," Becca said.

"Kassy went to a friend's house after school and won't be home till eight," her mother told her, "so supper is up to you." She paused. "When I get back, your dad and I would like to have a little family council with you girls."

"What about?" asked Becca.

Her mom glanced at Alvaro. "We'll talk about it when I get home, all right? And now," she added, picking up her briefcase from under the hall table, lightly kissing Alvaro on the top of the head, and blowing a kiss to Becca, "I really do have to run. Love you!"

The door closed behind her mother, and Becca ambled into the kitchen. She washed her hands at the sink, wiped her scraped leg with a clean dishcloth, then rummaged in the pantry and put a bag of pretzels on the kitchen table in front of Alvaro. "Come on, Jar-Jar. Have something to eat."

"Jar-Jar?" he asked around a mouthful of pretzel.

"It's a long story," Becca told him, gently ruffling his black hair. "You probably wouldn't understand." She watched as he crammed more food in his mouth. "If you keep eating like that, you'll look like Jabba the Hutt." She knew he wouldn't, though. Years of malnutrition had left Alvaro looking more like a four-year-old than the six-year-old he really was. Becca doubted whether he'd ever really had enough to eat before a medical missions team had arranged for him to come to the United States for surgery at the end of July. Lightly, she caressed the puckered skin on Alvaro's left arm.

"Sorry, buddy," she said as he flinched. The burns on Alvaro's arm were healed, so she knew he wasn't drawing back in pain. Becca guessed he was just fearful any time someone touched his scars. She didn't blame him. If she'd ever had serious thoughts about reshaping her too-big nose some day, what she'd learned about plastic surgery during their time as Alvaro's host family had convinced her that she could live with her nose the way God made it. And before the plastic surgery—which still hadn't made his arm and leg look normal—Alvaro had undergone skin grafts on most of his left side. He'd been through a lot—and that was just the medical side of things. Becca didn't want to imagine what it had been like for him to be caught in the fire that destroyed his home and killed his mother.

Becca sighed. *But you've put us through a lot, too, Alvaro. I know you can't help it, but you've really messed up our family while you've been here.*

"Come on, Alvaro," she said aloud. "Let's see if *Blue's Clues* is on. You can leave the Cheerios here."

Clutching the cereal box tighter, Alvaro followed her to the family room.

Half an hour later Becca had sat through about all the children's programming she could take. "Hey, Al," she said, clicking off the TV, "what do you say we go outside?" Becca walked across the backyard, kicking off her shoes as she went and balancing briefly on first one foot, then the other, to peel off her socks. She sat at the edge of the swimming pool and dangled her feet in the water. Dipping a finger in the pool, she flicked droplets across the smooth surface of the water, watching ripples spread and intersect. Idly, she wondered what tonight's family council would be about. Maybe they'd make plans to go away for a weekend after Alvaro left.

Last year they'd had a family council when her dad got a promotion. That's when they decided to take the extra money and put in a pool. Becca's dad had warned the kids that maintenance would be their job, but as far as Becca was concerned, it was worth it. Her house had been a hangout spot for her friends as long as she could remember. The pool was one more attraction. *Like the air hockey table*, Becca thought with a snort of disgust. *More fun than homecoming.*

Alvaro still stood on the patio just outside the door from the family room. Becca reached a hand toward him. "Come on! Want to swim? We don't get many warm days like this in October."

Alvaro shook his head.

"The pool's heated so it's real warm."

Alvaro shook his head harder.

"Just sit with me on the edge, then." Becca moved to take Alvaro's hand. "Just put your feet in."

"No! No!" Alvaro retreated until his back was against the sliding glass door. "No!" he said again, holding his Cheerios box up like a shield.

"Okay, Alvaro. We won't go in the water. Shhh. It's all right." Alvaro was getting more and more agitated. Mentally, Becca kicked herself. Why couldn't she just give it up? Nothing she did would help Alvaro lose his fear of the pool.

Not that she could blame him. Becca's mom had told the family about Alvaro's first day in the hospital. When the nurses lowered him into the whirlpool for hydrotherapy, he had screamed and screamed—a desperate, gasping wail that no child should ever have to make, Becca's mom said, her eyes filling with tears. She didn't know whether Alvaro was crying out in pain as the water sloughed off his burned skin, from sheer terror, or both. After they brought Alvaro home, they gave him sponge baths and even an occasional shower, but nothing could get him into the bathtub, much less the pool.

All right, swimming was out for today. What else could they do? Becca pulled a softball and two gloves out of the jumble of sports equipment in the bin on the patio.

"How about a game of catch? Good old American baseball." Gently, she began easing the smaller glove onto Alvaro's left hand. He didn't seem quite as jumpy about his scars as he had in the kitchen, but Becca took it slow just in case. Alvaro shifted the Cheerios box to his right arm and wiped his nose on his shirt sleeve. At least he didn't seem to be on the edge of hysteria anymore.

"We'll start with some easy ones." Becca tossed a slow, underhand throw. Alvaro watched it hit his glove and fall to the grass.

"Good try," Becca said. "Now you throw one to me."

As Alvaro bent for the ball, Cheerios spilled out of the open box. Squatting quickly, he closed the baseball glove over a little O in the grass, brought the glove to his mouth, then gaped in amazement to find it empty. Frowning in concentration, he tried again. And again. Becca began to giggle, then laugh out loud. At last Alvaro's eyes widened as if struck by a new thought, and he pulled off the glove.

"Atta boy!" Becca cheered. "You don't give up, do you?" Dropping to the ground beside him, she picked up a Cheerio and rolled to her back.

"Watch this," she said, tossing the piece of cereal into the air and trying to catch it in her mouth. It bounced off her forehead into the grass. Alvaro snatched it up and put it in the box.

"All right," Becca said, "I won't play with your food if you won't tell my mom that I let you eat off the dirt."

Tilting her head back, she studied the clouds. Fluffy, not wispy, she noted. Solana would know the scientific terms—cumulus as opposed to . . . something else. Whatever these clouds were called, to paragliders they signaled that the conditions were right for thermals—updrafts of hot air that an experienced pilot could catch and ride for 45 minutes or more. Becca had heard stories of pilots who stayed up for hours. She sighed. After 25 flights under the supervision of an instructor, she was now certified to go solo, but she was still a long way from experienced. She hadn't even been paragliding under thermal conditions yet, though she was itching to try. This afternoon would have been perfect.

Rolling over, she watched as Alvaro popped the last of the fallen Cheerios into his mouth. Had she given up the volleyball team so she could watch Alvaro dig for cereal in the dirt? She didn't mind helping her mom once in a while. But today was so perfect to do *something!* She hated sitting still more than anything.

"Alvaro, my man," she declared, standing and brushing bits of grass off her shirt, "you have got to learn to have fun."

Looking around for something that might appeal to him, Becca's glance fell on the hose coiled on its rack at the back of the house. When she and Matt and Kassy were little kids, they loved running through the sprinkler. Shoot, Becca still liked it. On the Fourth of July she and Solana had set up an obstacle course that covered most of the backyard, and all their friends and Kassy's and even Matt's had a blast leaping over the sprinkler, dodging water-bombs, sliding on the plastic runway, and finally doing cannonballs into the pool—all while members of the opposing teams shot them with super-soakers to slow them down.

I'd better try something tamer with Alvaro, Becca decided as she uncoiled the hose and attached a sprinkler. Not the one that spun around—she had a scar herself from the time she'd gotten tangled in the hose and fallen into those whirling arms. She found the sprinkler with the pierced tube that rotated back and forth, sending up a gentle arc of water like a rainbow.

Alvaro would surely balk if she tried to get him to wear a swimming suit. She didn't want him to associate this with his whirlpool experience. There were worse things than getting their clothes wet, Becca decided. Turning the water on low, she darted through the arch of water.

"Try it," she urged Alvaro. "Look—if you time it right, you don't even get wet."

She ran back and forth a few more times, sometimes staying dry, sometimes deliberately running through the water. Alvaro watched her with a guarded look. They probably didn't have sprinklers in the barrio where he came from, Becca decided.

The phone rang inside the house and Becca dashed to get it. "Be right back, Alvaro. Don't go in the pool." *At least that's one thing I don't have to worry about*, she thought.

As usual, the cordless phone was missing from its cradle in the family room. Becca lifted the couch cushions, sifted rapidly through an untidy pile of magazines, and checked on the fireplace mantle. By the fourth ring, she gave up and ran to the kitchen for the wall phone.

"Hello, you've reached the McKinnon's. We can't—" Becca snatched up the phone and interrupted the answering machine. "Hi. This is a real live McKinnon speaking."

"Hi, Becca. It's Jacie."

"Oh. Hi." Becca felt unexpectedly embarrassed as she recalled how abruptly she'd left the group at school. *I hate this!* she thought desperately. *Jacie is one of my best friends! I've always been able to talk to her about anything. But now if she asks me to explain why I was upset, I won't know what to say*. But as usual, Jacie wasn't asking, she was giving.

"Becca, I'm really sorry about what happened this afternoon. Tyler didn't mean to mess up anything between you and Nate; I know he didn't."

"Well—I guess there really isn't anything between me and Nate to mess up," Becca admitted.

"And with Tyler and me running your social life, there probably never will be," Jacie suggested, and Becca wondered if Jacie could read her mind.

"I don't even know if I *want* anything to happen with Nate," Becca confessed.

"Of course you do," Jacie interrupted. "We all see how you look at him."

Becca felt herself blush. "Really, I don't know for sure. That's why I wanted to go out in a group. I'm not ready for a boyfriend or anything serious like that."

"I know," Jacie said. "I thought I was when I started seeing Damien, but I guess that was a mistake . . ."Jacie's voice trailed off wistfully.

"Is that why you don't want to go to homecoming?" Becca asked. "Because of Damien?" Jacie had dated Damien secretly at the beginning of the school year. None of the close group of friends even knew about it until Hannah unearthed a painting of Damien in Jacie's studio and entered it in the art show without Jacie's knowing. Jacie and Damien practically broke up over that painting. Now they were friends again, but they had decided not to date—for now at least. And somehow Becca couldn't picture

Damien going to homecoming with their group of friends. He was too much of a loner.

"Oh, that's part of it, I guess," Jacie sighed. Becca knew it was taking lots of willpower for Jacie to be without Damien. "Mostly I was thinking of Hannah," Jacie continued. "In spite of what she did, we have to do things that help us forgive her. I think making her a part of our group might help all of us. Besides, imagine how left out she'd feel sitting home on homecoming."

"If you guys get your way, I won't have to imagine it, will I?" Becca said. "I won't be going to homecoming either!" In a gentler voice, she went on, "Jacie, it's really sweet how you want to help Hannah get started at school. But don't you think it's time she finds some friends of her own?"

Jacie was silent for a moment. Finally she said, "I know. That's how I've been feeling. But maybe we're being too hard on her."

"Too hard on her? Jacie—look at all the stuff she's done. She keeps jumping in where she doesn't belong. She took your picture without asking—"

"I'm trying to forgive her, Becca."

"Well, fine. Go ahead and forgive her. That doesn't mean you have to be best friends with her," Becca said. "Be honest, Jacie. Do you really have any fun with Hannah? Does she like to do any of the stuff we like to do? Do you really even like her?"

"I'm trying to like her," Jacie said slowly. "Becca, she's a *Brio* Sis. When you think about it, what's the right thing to do?"

"The *right* thing?" Becca stopped. What could she say? *We've been friends since fourth grade, and I don't need any new friends? I like our group the way it is and I'm afraid Hannah will change it? You've always cared for me and I'm afraid I'll get left out if you decide you'll care more for Hannah?* She couldn't think of any way to put her feelings into words without sounding selfish.

Slowly, explaining as much to herself as to Jacie, Becca said, "I thought this year was going to be the best one ever. Freshman and sophomore years, I was always Matt McKinnon's little sister. He was the best at everything, and I was always in his shadow. This was going to be my year to really go places on my own." Becca paused, waiting for Jacie to say something. Jacie was silent, so Becca continued. "But it turns out I really *miss* Matt! And instead we've got Alvaro, and he needs all kinds of attention, so it's like I'm in *his* shadow. And now Hannah's hanging around, and *she* needs all kinds of attention because she's new and has so many restrictions," Becca paused for air, "and I feel like all I ever do is take care of Alvaro, and now you want me to take care of Hannah, too."

Becca stopped abruptly. She hadn't meant to dump all this on Jacie. She didn't even know she felt this way till she heard herself saying it. Uncomfortably, she wondered what Jacie was thinking. Putting her feelings into words made them sound really selfish.

"Becca," Jacie said in a quiet tone that suggested she was working up to something important, "not everyone has a life like yours. Not everyone has plenty of money, the perfect family, and parents who give them lots of freedom. Some people have to live within restrictions and do the best they can. Did you ever think that Hannah doesn't agree with all her restrictions? If you can't let go of some of your perfect life to help other people . . ." Jacie left the rest unspoken.

Becca felt about as high as a Cheerio in the dirt. Jacie hated conflict, so for her to talk like that she must feel pretty strongly. Did she really think Becca was a spoiled brat? Worse, was she right?

A howl from outdoors cut into Becca's thoughts. Alvaro!

"Oh, Jacie—I've got to go," she blurted into the phone, and hung up. What if Alvaro had ventured into the pool after all? She didn't even know if he could swim!

chapter 

Racing outside, Becca quickly scanned the pool. No Alvaro. Instead, he was crouching, drenched to the skin, a few feet from the sprinkler, the disintegrating cardboard of the Cheerios box cradled in his arms and a puddle of soggy cereal at his feet. Every time the spray of water hit him, Alvaro let out another howl, but he persisted in trying to pick up each little O from the ground.

It took Becca till suppertime to get Alvaro cleaned up and calmed down. Her biggest worry was how he would handle the loss of his Cheerios. She hated the way he carried that box around all the time, like he was some weird refugee from an asylum run by General Mills, and she would be happy to see it gone. But when she tried to peel away the slimy cardboard strips that were the remains of the box, Alvaro held on with such desperation that Becca finally went to the pantry in search of a substitute.

She started to feel a little panicky herself when she realized they were out of Cheerios, but after sampling a few marshmallow stars and clovers, Alvaro accepted Lucky Charms as a substitute.

After supper—frozen pizza and chips, with a few baby carrots thrown on the plates as a concession to the food pyramid—Becca's dad handed Becca the Spanish Bible storybook they'd been using for family devotions ever since Alvaro had come to live with them. Becca, by virtue of being in her third year of Spanish at school, was the designated reader. At first Alvaro hadn't seemed too interested, but lately he'd paid close attention to the stories about Joseph. Maybe it was the 12 kids that interested him, Becca thought—the same size as Alvaro's family in Guatemala.

"Well, Becca, you cooked, so I'll clean up," Becca's dad offered, throwing away the paper plates and tossing the Coke cans in the recycle bin. "There!" he said, dusting his hands on his pants. "That's done!"

"Very generous, Dad," Becca replied. "Since I went to school today, would you like to do my homework?"

"Not likely!" he answered. "I want you to stay on the honor roll, and who knows what grades you'd get if I took over! But I'll put Alvaro to bed so you can hit the books."

From her desk in her bedroom, Becca could hear the water running as her dad got ready to sponge-bathe Alvaro's sutures. She hadn't mentioned Alvaro's shower earlier in the day; even if she had, her dad would want to check that everything was healing the way it should. Then he'd need to change the one remaining dressing on Alvaro's thigh where the infection kept coming back, and put medicated ointment on the skin grafts to keep the skin flexible. After that, check that the night-lights were on, tuck Alvaro into bed, rub his back until he fell asleep, and hope that tonight would be the night he'd sleep through without nightmares or wetting the bed.

"Becca!" the call came from the bathroom. "Can you come here a minute?"

Alvaro was perched on the bathroom counter, dressed only in underwear with pictures of dinosaurs on them. With all his scars exposed, his bony shoulder blades protruding, and the strange variation in skin tones over the areas that had been burned, he looked grotesque.

Wow, Jar-Jar, you really are an alien, Becca thought. *What if Hannah could see you now—wouldn't that be "special?"*

"I ran out of gauze," her dad said. "Can you get me some more from the medicine cabinet? I've got my hands full here."

Becca found the gauze quickly—the medicine cabinet was the one thing in the house her mother insisted everyone keep neat—and brought it to her dad.

"Cut me a piece about three inches long, will you?" he said, holding out his right hand for the gauze while keeping his left pressed against the bandage on Alvaro's thigh. When Becca handed him the gauze, he lifted the bandage. Chartreuse pus oozed out like guts from a squashed caterpillar. Becca's stomach lurched for her throat and she swallowed hard to fight it back down.

"How can you do that?" she asked, averting her eyes while her dad gently wiped away the pus.

"Gross, isn't it," he agreed, wrinkling his nose. "But that's what you do for someone you love." He cocked his head toward the door. "You can go back to your homework now. I'll take it from here. Thanks for the help."

● ● ●

Becca still had three algebra problems to do when she heard the garage door open. She glanced at her watch. Mom was home. Time for the family council. Good. She headed for the stairs and started to bound down them, then slowed to a walk when she remembered that thuds on the steps were enough to make Alvaro wake up screaming.

Kassy was already in the kitchen, telling Mom about the latest project she and her friends were into. Becca's dad sat at the table with a newsletter from the medical missions agency.

"Hey," Kassy said, as Becca walked in, "you're wearing your hair down."

"Yeah," Becca said, pulling it all over one shoulder. "What do you think?" Kassy was only in seventh grade, but she was already more in tune with styles than Becca ever hoped to be.

Kassy tilted her head to one side and studied Becca. "Good," she pronounced, "only you should part it a little more to the side."

"Both my girls are gorgeous," their dad said, putting away the newsletter and standing up to pull Becca and Kassy into a bear hug.

"You *are* attractive girls," their mother began, "but remember—"

Becca and Kassy looked at each other. "It's character that counts," they recited in unison, rolling their eyes.

"Well, it is," their mother replied mildly. "I'd rather you were beautiful on the inside than on the outside."

"Sermon over, Mom?" Kassy asked.

"Till next time," she smiled.

Mr. McKinnon returned to his chair at the table and motioned for the others to sit down.

"Your mom and I didn't call this family council to talk about hairstyles," he said, "as important as that might be. We wanted to give you an update on Alvaro." He looked at Mrs. McKinnon. She nodded and picked up the story.

"I got a call from the agency today. They've been in contact with Alvaro's father, of course, while Alvaro has been here—keeping him up to date on Alvaro's progress and so on. Well, it seems that Alvaro's father is overwhelmed with the prospect of taking care of Alvaro and his ongoing medical needs. When Alvaro's mother died in the fire that burned Alvaro," Becca's mother's voice shook, "the other 11 children were parceled out to the aunts and cousins. But," she took a deep breath, "it seems that no one wants Alvaro."

The girls were silent a moment. Then Becca spoke up. "That's terrible! What will happen to him?"

"He'll be sent to an institution," her dad answered, "unless someone adopts him."

"Poor Alvaro," Becca said. "You know how awful some of those orphanages can be." They had been so horrified by the stories of poverty and neglect her dad brought back from his last missions trip that they had decided to sponsor a child in a Honduran orphanage. Becca doubted that an orphanage in the slums of Guatemala City would be any better.

Kassy seemed to be thinking the same thing. "Could we sponsor Alvaro?" she asked.

Their dad looked from Kassy to Becca. "Sponsoring him might help," he said slowly, "but Alvaro's best hope would be adoption."

"Maybe," said Becca. "But don't most people want babies when they adopt? Who's going to adopt a scarred six-year-old who wets his bed at night?"

"We might," said Becca's mom. "We think we might."

In the few moments after her mother's announcement, Becca knew what the expression "deafening silence" meant. If somebody didn't say something soon—preferably something like, "Just kidding"—Becca thought her eardrums would burst.

She looked from her mother's face—eyebrows slightly raised, a gentle smile on her lips, her eyes gleaming with moisture—to her father's. He too was looking at Becca as if he expected her to break the silence. Becca glanced over at Kassy for help. Kassy looked the way Becca felt: blank and slightly stupid.

At last Becca gave the only response she could think of.

"You're not serious—are you?" It came out as a kind of croak.

"We're very serious," her dad replied. "This is a decision that could change Alvaro's life."

No kidding! Becca thought. *What about my life?*

Kassy spoke up. "Where would he sleep?" she asked abruptly. "You wouldn't give him my room, would you?" she pursued. "I wouldn't have to share with Becca?"

"No, you girls wouldn't have to give up your rooms," their mother assured them. "Alvaro would probably have the same room he's in now."

"But that's Matt's room!" Becca burst out. "Matt goes off to school and you just take away his room? What's he supposed to do, live on campus all summer?"

"We can finish a room in the basement for Matt," Becca's dad said in what she supposed was meant to be a soothing voice. "We'll ask Matt how he feels about it, of course. But you know that Matt isn't going to be home much anymore. Having Alvaro in the family won't make as much difference to him as it does to you girls. That's why we're talking with you first."

Kassy seemed satisfied. *As if her precious room is all that matters,* Becca thought. She opened her mouth to make a sarcastic reply, then shut it again. Sarcasm wouldn't help.

"I just don't think it would work," she began tentatively. "I mean, think of how much it would slow our family down to have a little kid around. Do you think he could keep up on the kinds of vacations we like to take? Can you see him carrying a backpack or going white-water rafting like we did last year?"

Becca's mom started to speak, but Becca quickly went on. "It's not just the fun stuff I'm thinking about! What about you and Dad? Any time you wanted to go out, you'd have to get a babysitter." Better make it clear that she and Kassy weren't going to be on call around the clock! She didn't need a regular routine of afternoons like the one she'd spent today. "And what about his medical problems? Can you keep taking off work to drive back and forth to Denver?"

"I really haven't missed that much work," Becca's mom replied. "I've been able to fit in my 20 hours around Alvaro's appointments. But I think I could arrange for a leave of absence from the community center if I need to."

"Mom!" Becca couldn't believe what she was hearing. Her mom would move mountains for the center. "If Alvaro's own family doesn't care enough about him to take care of him, why should you mess up your life to take him in?"

"Wait a minute, Becca!" her dad interjected. "Don't go judging Alvaro's family so fast. You don't know what they're up against." He paused. "It's possible that Alvaro's father doesn't care about him, I suppose," he continued soberly, "but it's probably not that simple. Parents in developing countries love their children just as much as we love ours. But Alvaro's father doesn't have many choices. He probably thinks Alvaro will have a better life this way."

Becca bit her lip. It wasn't that she didn't want Alvaro to have a good family. But did it have to be *her* family?

"I've been thinking about the story of Joseph you've been reading to Alvaro at suppertime," Becca's dad continued. "All those terrible things that happened to Joseph—his brothers abandoning him, becoming a slave, getting thrown in prison—God used all those things to bring Joseph to the place where God wanted him."

Becca and Kassy looked at their father blankly. Why was he telling Bible stories now?

"Well, I've been thinking," he went on, as if answering their unspoken question. "Could it be that God used the terrible experiences Alvaro's been through to bring him to us?"

Kassy's eyes narrowed as if she were trying to follow this reasoning, then opened wide. "Dad," she said slowly, "when Joseph was in Egypt, all his brothers came and joined him there. You aren't thinking of adopting all 11 of Alvaro's brothers and sisters too, are you?"

Mr. McKinnon laughed. "No, Kassy," he said, "we're only asking you to accept one brother."

"I already have a brother!" Becca's words came out fast now. "My brother was MVP on the basketball team last year, remember? He was salutatorian and senior class VP and on the homecoming court. My brother is smart and funny and fun to be around. He's not puny and weird and scared. Just because he's away at college, do you think I don't know what a *real* brother is like?"

"This isn't about replacing Matt," Becca's mom said gently.

"It's about a home for Alvaro." She leaned forward to look into Becca's eyes. "Becca, we don't love Matt because of all the things he's good at. We love him because he's part of our family. We love him the way God loves us—unconditionally. And that's the way we love Alvaro—even if he is 'puny and weird and scared.'" She smiled at Becca, but Becca didn't smile back.

"That's not love!" Becca said. "That's pity."

As soon as she said it, she wished she could call the words back. Her mother pulled away as if Becca had slapped her. Becca slumped back in her chair and looked down at her hands knotted in her lap. She was sorry she'd hurt her mom, but she couldn't apologize. She was too shaken by a new thought. Could it be that her mother really loved Alvaro the way she loved her own son? The way she loved Becca?

"Well, girls," her father finally said, "we won't try to make this decision tonight. Think about it, and pray about it, and we'll talk more about it another time."

"Why don't we pray together now?" her mom said, joining hands with her husband and Kassy.

As Kassy and her dad reached to take Becca's hands, Becca shoved back her chair and rushed out of the room. She wasn't about to get prayed into agreeing with this decision. Praying could be dangerous—in more ways than one. Getting thrown off her bike was something she could handle; letting God talk her into adopting Alvaro was a different matter.

chapter 4

The next day at school, Becca made a dash for the cafeteria as soon as the bell for first lunch rang. Usually all her friends ate together, but today Jacie was taking Hannah to a meeting for the school newspaper and Tyler had plans to eat with some of his friends from the basketball team. So it would be just Solana and Becca today, which was fine with Becca. If ever she needed a non-judgmental ear, it was now. Dumping her backpack on a table and getting in the Pizza Hut line, she wished for the millionth time that upperclassmen were allowed to leave campus during lunch. True, with its fast food kiosks, the cafeteria was more like a food court than a school lunchroom, but today Becca would gladly have traded her personal pan pizza for the chance to hold a private conversation. She scanned the rapidly filling cafeteria for Solana, hoping she'd get there before someone else sat at the table Becca had dumped her books on.

"Yo! Becca! Where are we sitting?" Solana called over the noise of the cafeteria.

Becca gestured to the table she'd saved, waited for her change, then sat down across from Solana.

"I hope you're feeling brilliant today," she told Solana, "because I sure need help!"

"Brilliance is my specialty," Solana said, taking a bottle of sparkling lime water out of her lunch bag and twisting off the cap. "What's the problem? Nate and the elusive homecoming date?" She grinned. "You've come to the right place. Guys are *really* my specialty."

"Yeah, well some of that knowledge I can live without," Becca said. "Anyway, I have a bigger problem now." She picked up a slice of pizza, then set it down again. "Hang on a second." Becca closed her eyes for a quick silent prayer, then looked up and reached for her pizza.

"When are you going to stop doing that?" Solana asked with a hint of exasperation in her voice.

"Doing what?"

"That prayer thing," Solana answered. "You ought to be more consistent, you know. If you really believe God is going to help you, why bother to ask me for help? Or, to put it another way, why bother with God when you've got brilliant me?"

Becca sighed. "There are days when I almost think you're right."

Solana raised her eyebrows. "A crisis of faith? Becca, you surprise me."

"No, not a crisis of faith," Becca answered. "Just a crisis. You'll never believe what my parents are thinking about doing." She told Solana about the family council the night before.

"Hunh," Solana murmured. She gazed at the cafeteria wall as if her eyes were focused on something else.

Becca waited a few moments in silence, then said, "*Hunh?* That's all your brilliance has to offer? Just *hunh?*"

"I was thinking," said Solana. "I wish someone had given Marisa a chance like that."

"Marisa!" Becca exclaimed. "Who in the world is Marisa?"

Solana refocused on Becca. "Marisa was my best friend in Colima, Mexico. I never told you about her . . ." Solana's voice drifted off and she sighed. Then she looked into the distance as if she could see her memories. "I used to play with her every summer when we went to visit my *abuela*—my grandmother." Solana's whole body seemed to stiffen as she talked. "The summer Marisa and I were 10, she died of hepatitis. Hepatitis, Becca!" Solana raised her voice. "In America, nobody has to die of hepatitis! Even poor babies can get vaccinated for free at the county health department. But in Mexico all they could do for Marisa was pray." Solana spat the word "pray" out as if she could hardly stand the taste it left in her mouth.

Becca reached across the table and put her hands over Solana's. "Solana, I'm so sorry. You could have told me."

Solana turned her hands palm up to give Becca's a quick squeeze before pulling away. "I know. It wasn't something I felt like talking about." She leaned forward to look at Becca intently. "But if someone had given Marisa the chance your family is giving Alvaro, she'd still be alive."

Becca felt for a minute like a deer caught in somebody's headlights. She sat there, returning Solana's intense gaze while she tried to think of something to say. Finally she broke eye contact. "Yikes, Solana, you make it sound so dramatic. I don't really think Alvaro's situation is a matter of life and death anymore."

Solana looked at her pointedly. "You don't know that." She paused to take a bite of cold tamale. "I mean it, Becca—even if Alvaro's life wasn't on the line anymore, your family has a chance to do something really awesome for Alvaro."

"I guess," Becca said. "Nothing's settled yet."

Solana seemed to sense that Becca had had enough of the subject. "Speaking of settled, we haven't decided what we're doing for the weekend," she said. "Got any ideas?"

"Well, you could come with me to the homeless shelter tomorrow. They always need extra help with the kids on Saturdays," Becca teased. She'd been pestering her friends to get involved in the shelter at the community center for months, but so far no one had taken her up on it.

"Kids! Human larvae, you mean!" Solana replied. "Give me foals any day!"

"It's only once a month," Becca persisted. "The other Saturdays are covered." She grinned. "I just thought I'd remind you of the opportunity."

"Uh-huh," nodded Solana. "In case the monthly e-mail notice you send isn't enough of a memory jogger."

"Exactly," Becca said.

"I'm telling you, Becca," Solana said, "you ought to be more consistent. You get all worked up about social justice and caring for the poor, but only when you can keep it at arm's length and do it once a month."

"Ouch," said Becca. "Say what you really think once in a while, why don't you?" She looked for a way to redirect the conversation. "Want to trade that tamale for my pizza? I'd take your mom's leftovers over Pizza Hut any day."

"No, but you can admire it all you want," Solana said, sticking out a tongue full of chewed food. She looked at the clock on the wall and crammed the rest of the tamale in her mouth. "Eat if you're going to. We've gotta go."

● ● ●

The bell rang as Becca and Solana headed out of the cafeteria, Solana grasping Becca's arm and swinging her to the left as Becca turned right into the hallway.

"*This* way to English class," she reminded Becca.

"Oh, yeah," Becca grinned. "I knew that."

Katie Spencer fell into step with them as they climbed the stairs to the second floor. "Hi, Becca, Solana. Did you lose the Mormon?"

"Mormon?" Becca repeated. "What do you mean?"

"Or Quaker, or whatever she is," Katie answered. "That new girl with the prude clothes you're always hanging around with lately."

"Oh!" Becca caught on. "Hannah Connor."

"Gee, Katie," said Solana, "could you be a little more superficial? What's it to you how the girl dresses?"

Katie raised her eyebrows at Solana. "Sorry!" she said with exaggerated politeness. Turning to Becca, she explained, "I was just surprised to see you hanging with her, that's all. She seems more like the Betty Crocker Club type." Katie shrugged and moved down the hall as Becca and Solana turned into their English classroom.

Hannah walked into class just as Becca was settling into her desk. Becca wondered how many people besides Katie thought she was hanging out with Hannah by choice. The Betty Crocker Club was about as uncool as you could get at Stony Brook High. Not that Becca wanted to be superficial or put down anyone who was into the domestic stuff—but Hannah did look as if she'd fit right in with that particular club. Maybe she should suggest that Hannah join. Then Hannah would have a group of her own and she and her friends could get back to normal.

"May I sit by you?" Hannah asked softly, smiling tentatively at Becca.

"Oh, sure," Becca said, feeling suddenly as if all her unkind thoughts were printed on her forehead for Hannah to read. Quickly she turned her attention to Mr. Garner at the front of the room.

Sitting on the edge of his desk with one khaki-clad leg crossed over the other, Mr. Garner grinned and said, "Thanks for all the papers on the structure of the short story. I don't have them all graded yet, but I'll try to get them back to you on Monday." He shot a glance at a couple of students slouching in the back corner. "Andy. Rafe. You want your papers back on Monday, you hand them in to me today. Got it?"

He leaned forward and continued, "We're going to leave the short story now and move on to something new—a play: *The Diary of Anne Frank*."

"Man," grumbled Rafe, "I read that book when I was in seventh grade."

"Great!" replied Mr. Garner. "Then you've probably got some idea about why I want you to read the play." When Rafe shook his head, Mr. Garner looked around the room. "Anybody?"

"Because it's the school play this year and you're directing it?"

said one of the girls near the front.

"Yeah, that's part of it," Mr. Garner agreed. "If it's worth doing as a play—and believe me, it is—it's worth reading in advance. Any other ideas?" He stood up and started pacing, and Becca and Solana exchanged smiles. Mr. Garner could never stay still very long—he got too excited about his subject. That was one of the reasons almost all the students—even kids like Andy and Rafe, who tended to be slackers in other teachers' classes—liked him so much.

"Okay," he said, holding his hand up as if to frame a movie scene, "*Anne Frank*—the play version, anyway—is a drama, not so different from a good movie or TV show. A *good* movie or TV show," he repeated with emphasis. "What do you look for in a good drama?"

A girl in the front row raised her hand, and Mr. Garner stopped pacing and pointed at her.

"Romance," she cooed, flipping her hair and looking up at him through her eyelashes. Several of the guys near the back of the room snorted, and one called out, "Lust!" but she went on. "How about *you*, Mr. Garner? You're a single man. Are you looking for romance?"

"Bonnie," Mr. Garner said, shaking his head, "I'm selective. But," he went on, "if it's romance you're looking for in a drama," he looked at the back of the room, "or even lust, you'll find it in this play."

Becca noticed several of the girls opening their copies of *Anne Frank* with new interest, but beside her Hannah seemed to stiffen defensively, her head down and her eyes focused on her desk.

"A good drama raises questions," Mr. Garner said, striding around the room. "Questions like, *How do you handle the drive for physical intimacy? How far should you go if you love someone? How far should you go if you don't love the person? How do you know if your parents' values are your values?* Have you ever asked questions like these?"

Becca caught Solana's eye. They talked about questions like this all the time. Becca noticed that Hannah was now looking up from her desk.

"OK—love and sex." Mr. Garner said. "Basic human drives with all sorts of personal, moral, and ethical issues. What else do you look for in drama?"

"Violence!" yelled one of the guys from the back. About half the class snickered while the other half turned as if to shout him down, but Mr. Garner interrupted.

"Exactly! Look at 9 of the top 10 movies playing, and I'll bet you'll find lots of violence. Whether or not that's a good thing is another question—and one we can talk about as we explore this play. But if you want violence, you'll get it in *Anne Frank*. Nazis. Air raids. Deportation at gunpoint. Death camps." He banged his desk explosively. "Violence gets our attention! And if we're thinking," he looked pointedly at the back corner, "it forces us to ask questions. Is violence avoidable? Is it necessary? Is it ever moral? Do you find it entertaining?"

In the uncomfortable pause that followed his last question, Mr. Garner sat down again on the edge of his desk. "And what about discrimination?" he asked. "Anne was a Jew living under the Nazi regime. Is the issue of how people judge others worth exploring?"

"You know it, Mr. Garner!" Rafe's hand shot up. "Go to the 7-Eleven, they watch you like an eagle. Like they think every Hispanic is a shoplifter."

A chorus of voices joined Rafe's.

"My brother," an African-American kid spoke up. "He got pulled over three times in one month—not even speeding. 'Suspicious vehicle,' the cops called it. Suspicious driver is what they meant. Dangerous male."

"Yeah, well, try being female! You wait tables and they'll pinch your butt and tell you you're supposed to like it."

"They call you loose."

"Call you lazy."

"Call you ignorant."

Mr. Garner rose and stood in front of his desk, his arms outstretched as if to wrap the room and every student in it in a huge embrace. Or, thought Becca suddenly, like a picture of Christ with his arms outstretched on the cross.

"So," he said softly as the room quieted, "like Anne Frank, you know what it is to be judged because of your race." Becca saw that nearly all the African-American and Hispanic students were nodding their heads, Solana among them.

"And some of you who haven't had to face racial discrimination know what it is to be judged for other things—how you look, how you dress, how you measure up to one standard or another."

Hannah was sitting up straight now, looking directly at Mr. Garner and nodding soberly. This time it was Becca who dropped her gaze to her desktop.

"We're going to spend the rest of this class period reading this play aloud. Rafe," Mr. Garner pointed at him, "you've encountered this story before, in book form. Now you're coming to it in a new genre—drama—and with, I hope, some new maturity. Will you read the part of Mr. Frank?"

Rafe sat straighter in his chair. "You've got it, Mr. Garner."

At the end of class, Becca stayed seated, her elbow on the desk and her fist pressed against her mouth. Hannah hesitated by her desk, then left the room with the other students.

"Uh-oh. What's bugging you?" Solana asked, as she scooped up her books and prepared to go to her next class. "I see you're in your thinker pose."

"I guess I'm just feeling ugly," Becca answered, as she gathered her own books and got up to leave.

"Ugly as in you think your nose is too big?" Solana queried. Becca's "thinker pose" had started in middle school as a way of camouflaging her profile, and she still fell into the habit when she was thinking hard.

"No, ugly inside," Becca said, as they started walking toward the door. "Solana, we've been best friends for ages, and all of a sudden today I felt as if we were in different worlds. I felt so strange to see you nodding your head about feeling discriminated against." Solana didn't say anything, so Becca kept talking. "I mean, of course I know you're Hispanic—"

"Bright girl," Solana teased.

"—but I never thought it made any difference. Wait, that doesn't sound right. I don't mean that it's not an important part of who you are. I mean . . . I don't know what I mean. Stop me, Solana! I'm babbling!"

"You mean it never occurred to you that people like me would feel discriminated against by people like you," Solana offered.

"Exactly!" Becca said in relief. "And now I feel like a jerk for having been so blind."

"So you learned something." Solana grinned. "I always said Mr. Garner is a pretty good teacher."

"I've been thinking about what you said over lunch," Becca said. "About Alvaro—and Marisa." She looked intently at Solana.

"I don't want you to think I don't want my parents to adopt Alvaro because he's Hispanic."

"*Mi amiga.*" Solana reached out and touched Becca gently on the shoulder. "I know you wouldn't reject Alvaro because he's Hispanic."

Becca smiled, grateful for Solana's understanding. As they separated to go to different classes though, Solana said, "No, it's not because he's Hispanic. I don't know why you're rejecting Alvaro."

● ● ●

The digital numbers glowed green in the dark—1:30. Becca turned her back to the clock and willed her body to relax, to fall asleep. But her mind kept going at drag-race speed. *Alvaro. Hannah. Nate.* Becca turned back to look at the clock—1:32. She couldn't just lie there much longer. She rolled out of bed and onto the floor and did 25 fast sit-ups. If she couldn't relax her body, maybe she could exhaust it. Next, jumping jacks. But after one jump she realized that jumping jacks make too much noise in a quiet house at 1:32—no, 1:34—in the morning.

She pulled open a drawer at her desk and rummaged through it to find her journal. Two back issues of *Brio* magazine, a folder of photos from summer vacation—she flipped through those for a minute—a receipt from the resale shop, and an index card with Matt's college address, but no journal. Someday she had to clean out her desk. But not tonight.

She zipped open her backpack and pulled out a spiral notebook and a pen. Flopping back down on her bed, she lay there for a minute, propped up on her elbows, fist pressed against her mouth. Then she flipped on the light on her nightstand, opened the notebook, and started to write.

How did everything get so out of control? It's like my whole life took a wrong turn and now I'm heading full speed in the wrong direction.

And I don't dare yell for help.

I'm supposed to have everything under control. I'm the one with the perfect family, the great friends, the fabulous life. So how do I dare tell anybody that it doesn't feel so perfect right now? That, to be honest, my family and friends are letting me down?

Somehow, being honest doesn't seem to work very well right now.

When I try to be honest with Mom and Dad about Alvaro, they look so hurt, so disappointed in me.

When I'm honest with Jacie about Hannah—I don't know, it's like she doesn't want to hear my side of it.

And Solana. I could always tell her anything, but right now I'm afraid everything I say might get all twisted up in questions of prejudice and judging and rejecting other people.

I'm even starting to wonder—can I be honest with you, God?

Because if I can, here's the truth: I

want my life back. The way it used to be.

Becca rolled over onto her back and looked up into the dark. *The way it used to be*. She got up, went to her desk, and picked up the stack of pictures from summer vacation—before Alvaro came. Before Hannah started school. She lay on her bed and looked at each picture in the glow of the alarm clock.

Mom and Dad, Becca, Matt, and Kassy white-water rafting. Everybody having fun; nobody screaming in fear of the water.

Tyler, Solana, Jacie, and Becca at a photo shoot at *Brio* magazine. Looking good, having a blast. Nobody disapproving or slowing them down.

Becca flipped through one picture after another. This was her life. The way it was supposed to be.

God? Are You listening?

chapter 5

"Rise and shine!"

Becca opened one eye to peer at her mother's cheerful face, then pulled her pillow over her head.

"Waffles in 15 minutes!" her mother chirped sweetly, as she snapped up the window shades with a flourish and waltzed out the bedroom door.

What did I do to deserve a mother who's a morning person? Becca wondered, as she calculated whether it was worth the effort to get out of bed and pull the shades back down.

Her mom poked her head back in the door. "Today's your center day! Don't forget!"

The community center. Becca sat up abruptly, a smile cracking the saliva on her cheek where she had drooled during the night. The community center was worth getting up for.

The Outreach Community Center had been part of Becca's life since she was nine years old, when her mom had started volunteering at the center three mornings a week. Within six months, the volunteer position had turned into a 20-hour-a-week paying job coordinating volunteer services. More than that, it had become Mrs. McKinnon's passion. "Don't bother Mom unless there's blood or fire," were the guidelines set down that first summer, when, with the kids out of school, she went off to work and left Becca and Kassy under 12-year-old Matt's supervision for the first time.

Matt's job as family baby-sitter lasted a week and a half, until one day a friend came by on his bike and invited him to ride down to the creek "for just a minute." The minute stretched into an hour or two, which was ample time for Becca to experiment with an aeronautical engineering device she'd been rigging up in her bedroom out of sheets, some old jumpropes, and several rolls of duct tape. She got up onto the roof with her makeshift parachute and took a long running start, but—fortunately or unfortunately, depending on the point of view—got tangled in the branches of the big aspen at the corner of the house.

There she hung, methodically trying to untangle the cords, until Kassy finally heard her intermittent calls and came out of the house, looked up, and saw her.

"Becca!" she shouted. "Is there blood?"

Receiving a negative response, she knew better than to disturb her mother. Instead, she went into the house and dialed 9–1–1. The first Mrs. McKinnon heard of the event was when a neighbor called her at the center to ask, "Do you know that there are fire trucks in front of your house?"

After that, Matt stayed home alone and Becca and Kassy accompanied their mother to the community center. When Becca outgrew the after-school and summer school programs, it just seemed natural to keep coming to the center as a volunteer. Sometimes she worked in the resale shop, either behind the counter or in the back room unloading and sorting through donations of clothing, housewares, and just about anything else that might be saleable. Other times she helped out in the food pantry.

But the place Becca felt most compelled to be was in the homeless shelter. The Outreach Community Center had begun providing meals and a place to sleep about a year ago, and when Becca first visited, she was astounded that there could be so many people without homes in her own community.

"Where were they before?" she asked her mom. "I never saw any homeless people before."

"No," her mother had answered, sounding sad. "Most people don't."

Becca hadn't understood at first, but now she thought she knew what her mom meant. Because now when she went to the downtown branch of the Copper Ridge Public Library, she often saw Mr. Anderson sitting quietly in the periodicals section—especially on cold days. Probably none of the other people in the library gave the old man with the long beard a second look, much less thought about whether he had a place to sleep at night. Sometimes when Becca was riding home from school, she'd see Gloria heading to the grade school to meet her kids, hauling a big plastic trash bag for any aluminum cans she might find on the way.

Becca made a point of learning the names of the people who used the shelter and saying hi to them when she saw them in other places. It made her feel good—as though she were connected to something bigger and more important than just her own routine of school and sports and friends. And maybe today it would help her get her mind off her own problems for a little while.

Hair still wet from the shower, Becca bounded into the kitchen. Kassy was already at the table, pouring syrup on a plate of waffles.

"Welcome to the Brady Bunch," she said to Becca, stabbing her fork in the general direction of their mother. "Mom seems to have gone all domestic on us today."

Mrs. McKinnon turned from the waffle iron to smile at Becca. She brushed a stray lock of hair off her forehead, leaving a smudge of waffle mix behind. Even at her most domestic, Mrs. McKinnon's efforts didn't go as far as making waffles from scratch.

"I thought it would be nice to have a good breakfast," she said with satisfaction. "Besides," she added, "we don't have anything in the house for lunch or supper, so I figure we may as well tank up. Let's see," she moved to the three-ring binder that housed the family calendar, school notices, appointment reminders, and so on. "Kassy, don't forget your flute lesson at 10 today. You'll have to bike over, because Dad and I will be at the foster parents' meeting going over Alvaro's current status. Becca, you can take my car to the center today. I'll need you to take Alvaro with you—will that be okay?"

Her tone changed from businesslike to hesitant, and Becca looked up to see her mother looking at her with an expression of concern. "Would you mind keeping track of Alvaro this morning, Honey?"

It's not like I never want to see the kid again, Becca thought, touched by her mother's concern but half exasperated too. *I just don't think I want us to adopt him.* Out loud, though, all she said was, "Sure, Mom. No problem."

"Great," her mom responded. "You're all on your own for lunch, and maybe tonight we'll go out to eat. Make sure Alvaro gets lunch, okay, Becca?"

"Sure," Becca said again. "Where is he, anyway?"

"In the driveway." Mrs. McKinnon pointed and Becca pushed aside the curtains to look out the window.

Alvaro was seated on the tricycle Mrs. McKinnon had brought home from the resale shop for him, his cereal box tucked firmly under one arm. He still had the Lucky Charms, Becca noted. He was wearing blue pants and a blue top with a red *S* emblazoned on his chest. He seemed to be adjusting the Velcro fastenings that held a red cape to his shoulders.

"Mom!" Kassy said, sounded scandalized. "He's outside in his *pajamas again!*"

"Um-hmm," agreed her mom. "I don't think he has a clue who Superman is, but he sure loves that cape. Watch."

Alvaro had apparently adjusted the Velcro to his satisfaction, because he faced forward and began peddling as fast as his skinny little legs could move. As soon as he picked up a little speed, he turned his head to admire the cape flowing out behind him. But when he turned his head, he turned his whole upper body, and the handlebars of the trike, too. Soon he was peddling furiously in tighter and tighter circles, looking like a scrawny little dog trying to catch its tail.

The three of them were laughing at the window when Mr. McKinnon joined them.

"Look at him go, Dad!" Becca said. "He sure loves speed!"

"Just like you," her dad replied. "I bet he'll love paragliding when he's older, too."

"He looks like he has Becca's sense of direction," chimed in

Kassy. "Going around in circles like he can't tell his left from his right."

But Becca was too lost in thought to notice Kassy's teasing. *Would Alvaro love paragliding? He would never get a chance in a Guatemalan orphanage, that's for sure. Was her dad already assuming that Alvaro was a permanent part of their family?*

"Oh, no!" Becca's mom cried suddenly. "The waffles!" Smoke and a very bad smell came from the waffle iron as she scraped out the blackened remains of what was to have been Becca's breakfast.

"You are certainly no Betty Crocker, dear," Becca's dad said, and Becca flinched guiltily, "but your other qualities more than make up for it." He cupped her face in both his hands and kissed the smudge of waffle mix on her forehead.

Kassy made a face at Becca, and Becca grimaced back. Her parents could be so corny sometimes. Not that she didn't appreciate their commitment to each other—divorce seemed to hang over everybody's head these days, and she was glad that her parents were serious about making their marriage last. Plenty of her friends didn't have that security. Jacie lived alone with her mom—her parents had never been married. Tyler's mom was awesome, but Becca could tell that their home was happier when Tyler's dad was away on business. Then there were kids like Alvaro—kids who would be better off in their home country, she told herself firmly, or who could find an adoptive home with a family that wasn't already perfectly happy the way they were.

And there were kids at the community center waiting for their breakfast, she remembered, so she'd better get a move on.

"I'll catch breakfast at the center," she told her mom. "I like eating with the people there. Besides," she added with an impish grin, "the cooks there are professionals." Dodging a swat from her mother's spatula, Becca grabbed the car keys from their hook by the side door and ran to the garage.

"Come on, Alvaro," she called. "You're coming with me today." As she hustled him toward the car, she realized he was still in his pajamas. "Think we should change your clothes quick?" she asked, tugging lightly on his cape.

A rare smile lit Alvaro's face, and he spread his arms and broke into a hobbling run. "Vooosh!" he said, unmistakably the sound of flight in either English or Spanish.

"Vooosh!" Becca echoed, and raced him to the car. *Let the kid go in his pajamas*, she decided. *If it gives him wings, he ought to have a chance to use them.*

"We're here, Alvaro," Becca sang out as she pulled into the Outreach Community Center parking lot. "My home away from home!"

"Home?" said Alvaro cautiously. *"Mi casa?"*

He'd begun picking up a little English during his stay with the McKinnons. But he seemed uncertain about the center right now. Of course! She'd confused him by calling it home. Who knew what *home* meant to Alvaro? His home in Guatemala was burned to the ground. For the last month they'd been calling Becca's house his home. In a week or two he was scheduled to go back "home" to Guatemala—did he know that his new home there might be an orphanage? Becca hadn't thought to ask her parents whether Alvaro knew that his father was putting him up for adoption. If he did know, it was no wonder he looked at the community center so warily.

"Never mind the 'home' part," she told him. "It was just an expression. It just means I love this place." And she did. She loved the way she felt as soon as she walked through the doors—this was a place where she belonged, where she could do something that really mattered. She felt the same rush that she got when she stepped onto the court for a big game.

Becca was untangling Alvaro's cape from the shoulder belt on his booster seat when she heard a car horn. She straightened up to see a familiar, metallic-green Toyota Tercel pulling into the parking space next to her.

"Jacie!" she cried delightedly as her friend bounded out of the front seat. "I can't believe you actually decided to come!"

"I can't believe I agreed to ride in that backseat," complained Tyler as he clambered out and made a show of stretching his arms and legs. "Jacie, your car is designed for midgets."

"You could have driven your own car if you were so concerned about leg room, instead of mooching Jacie's gas," Becca accused. But she beamed at Tyler. She'd been pestering her friends for months to join her, but they always had some excuse. Finally they'd come through for her—maybe things were looking up in the *Brio* group after all!

"I *offered* to drive," Tyler defended himself, "but Hannah could only come if Jacie picked her up."

Hannah. Becca had assumed Solana was in the front passenger's seat, but sure enough, the door opened and Hannah stepped out of the car.

"Not Solana?" Becca said stupidly.

"We're all here except Solana," Jacie answered, giving Becca a look she couldn't quite read.

"Hannah's parents are sure strict," Tyler murmured confidentially. "They'll hardly let Hannah do anything with a guy." Brightening, he added, "But they'll let her volunteer at the community center. That's no problem."

You're not here for me, Becca realized. *You're here for Hannah.*

"We're *all* here except Solana," Jacie repeated, widening her eyes and tilting her head slightly toward the Tercel.

Becca followed her gaze and felt her own eyes widen. Jackknifed in the backseat with his knees to his chin, waiting patiently for Hannah to unload a big bag of books, sat Nate Visser.

chapter 

"Yo, Becca!" Nate said, shaking out his long limbs and coming around to Becca's side of the car. "Hi, Superman," he added, smiling down at Alvaro, who quickly retreated behind Becca and clenched a fistful of her shirttail. "Where do we go to get started?"

"We'll go in the main entrance," Becca said, taking Alvaro's hand and leading the way across the parking lot. "The door directly to the homeless shelter is around the side, but there's something in the front lobby I want you to see."

Tyler reached out to take Hannah's bag from her. "Hey, what do you have in here, anyway?" he asked. "Bricks to build houses for the homeless?"

"No, just books," Hannah replied. "The e-mail said we'd be working with children, so I brought some books to read aloud."

Not a bad idea, admitted Becca grudgingly. She hadn't sent

Hannah her standard e-mail invitation to volunteer at the shelter, but she supposed Jacie had forwarded it to her. Jacie could be so undiscriminating about who she included. Still, she'd gotten Nate here, and that was worth something.

"Thanks," Becca said to Nate as he held the door open for the girls to enter the lobby.

"Thanks," she repeated under her breath to Jacie, looking over her shoulder to make sure Nate didn't hear.

"Don't thank me," Jacie whispered back. "It was Tyler's idea. I think he felt bad about the other day—you know, the homecoming thing." As Becca made an exasperated noise, Jacie added, "Give him a break—he's trying to make it up to you."

"Yeah, well, he's only here so he can spend time with Hannah, not because he cares about the homeless," Becca pointed out.

"And Nate's only here so he can spend time with you," Jacie shot back, eyes sparkling. "You have a problem with that?"

"None at all," agreed Becca. "None at all."

As Jacie walked through the door, she sucked in her breath. Becca nodded with satisfaction. "That's what I wanted you to see," she said.

Stretching the height and width of the lobby wall was a multidimensional fabric wall hanging. Babies with dimpled faces, old men with tangled yarn beards, boys and girls, and women and men were created out of fabric and old clothes. Larger than life and central to the piece was a smiling figure, arms outstretched and reaching from one end of the artwork to the other.

"Oh," exclaimed Jacie, "look! It's the name of the center, only visual. Outreach! Outreach Community Center."

Alvaro tugged on Becca's arm. "*José?*" he asked, pointing to the central figure.

"No," she answered. "Not Joseph. Jesus. But it does look like Joseph in our Bible storybook, doesn't it? Especially the part of the story when he hugs his brothers."

"That's how my youth pastor used to look when he said the blessing at the end of a service," Tyler said.

Jacie smiled and nodded, remembering. "I've seen him do it. He always reached his arms wide open, like he wanted to send a hug straight from God to the whole church."

"Uh," Tyler said. "I never really thought about it like that—"

"That's how Mr. Garner stood the other day in class," Becca remembered, "when people were talking about the ways they felt discriminated against." She flushed, suddenly feeling uncomfortable remembering that Hannah had been one of those who felt unfairly judged.

"I bet the bright fabrics remind Alvaro of Joseph's coat of many colors," Jacie said, moving toward the wall to read the sign. "What does this mean: 'Medium: gleaned fabric'?"

"All the fabric is leftovers or throwaways," Becca explained. "You know—'gleaned' like Ruth in the Bible did when she picked up the leftover grain from the edges of the fields. Look," she said, pointing at the figure of a small boy. "These are jeans I sold to the artist when he came into the resale shop."

"The fabric for these faces could have come from my parents' old bedsheets," observed Tyler.

"Ugh," Jacie shuddered. "Copper-colored sheets. I like them better as faces."

They moved along the sculpture, identifying stuffed gloves as hands, an apron made from a bandana, and even several pairs of mismatched gym shoes.

"Becca," Jacie finally said, "I think you belong in this sculpture. This is just how I see you: arms wide open—and wearing thrift shop clothes!"

Becca laughed and looked down at her khaki cargo shorts, raspberry plaid shirt, and fisherman's vest decorated with neon-colored trout flies. It was a standing joke that Becca, whose family had plenty of money, always shopped at the resale store, while Jacie, whose family had almost none, settled for nothing less than top-name brands from *Raggs by Razz* or one of the other fashionable clothing stores.

Becca leaned against the wall hanging and flung her arms wide. "Take a look! I fit right in!"

"You're a piece of work, all right, Becca," said Tyler, "if that's what you mean."

"Look at Alvaro," interrupted Hannah. "What's he doing?"

Alvaro had gone to one end of the sculpture and was stopping at each figure, peering at it intently and running his fingers over the wrinkled textures of the fabrics. From time to time he would look up at the Christ figure, then move methodically to the next fabric person.

"It's okay," Becca said. "This is the kind of art you can touch."

"I didn't mean that," replied Hannah. "I think he's looking for something." Quietly she crouched near the child and asked, "Alvaro, what are you looking for?"

Looking up, he replied, "Alvaro."

The friends were silent for a moment, then Becca, glancing at the clock on the adjacent wall, said, "Whoa! Guys, we've gotta get to work! Mrs. R. will be all over me if we're late!"

"Who's Mrs. R?" Nate asked as Becca jogged ahead of them down the hall.

"Mrs. Robeson. She runs the shelter—the Saturday shift, anyway—and believe me, nothing gets past her," Becca answered as she ushered her friends to a medium-sized room filled with tables and chairs.

"Becca!" exclaimed a gray-haired woman in a purple T-shirt with "Outreach Community Center" screen-printed on the sleeve. "Am I glad to see you! We're a little behind schedule, as you can see." She glanced at her watch. "So are you," she added.

"Sorry, Mrs. R.! But I brought reinforcements." Quickly Becca turned to her friends. "Jacie-Tyler-Nate-Hannah," she rattled off in a single breath, "this is Mrs. Robeson. Mrs. Robeson, these are—"

"Yes, I heard their names, Becca. And who is this?" she asked, pointing to Alvaro. "One of the clients? He shouldn't be taking food out of the kitchen." She looked pointedly at Alvaro's Lucky Charms box.

"No, Mrs. R., this is Alvaro. I thought you'd met him with my mom."

Mrs. Robeson took a closer look at Alvaro. "Oh, of course. I remember now. Because of the pajamas I thought he'd spent the night here. Well," she continued, "you know the ropes, Becca. Get the tables set for the second shift and then you can show your friends what else needs to be done." She walked briskly to the kitchen.

"First we clear everything off the tables," Becca directed, sweeping paper napkins into a large trash barrel while Alvaro trailed behind her, holding tight to her shirttail. "Two of you can grab those buckets and follow behind us, wiping the tables. Then we need to set every table with napkins, cups, and silverware—eight settings per table."

"What about plates?" Jacie asked.

"We'll bring those out with the food already on them once everyone's seated," Becca explained.

"It looks as though they've already had breakfast," Tyler observed as he wiped up some syrup with a wet rag.

"The shelter doesn't have enough space for everyone to eat at the same time," Becca explained, "so breakfast is served in two shifts."

Soon the tables were all cleared and wiped, and Becca glanced at the clock. She liked to race against her fastest table-setting time. None of the clients had to wait a minute longer than necessary for their breakfast on her shift. "Ready, set, go!" she murmured under her breath, and spun around to race for the clean silverware. Instead, she ran right into Alvaro and knocked him to the floor.

"Sorry!" she said, and scooped him up, but he sagged in her arms and refused to stand up. "Come on, Alvaro. We have work to do!" Alvaro sniffed, then began whimpering, but he didn't stand. Becca glanced again at the clock. Shoot! By this time she usually had half the tables set. She set Alvaro on the floor, but before she could walk away he had latched onto her ankle, anchoring her to the spot. *Now what?* Becca thought. *How does Mom handle it when he gets clingy?*

Becca bent down and slung Alvaro on her hip. He was small and skinny for his age, so his weight wouldn't slow her down much. But holding Alvaro left her only one hand for setting the tables.

"Hey, Alvaro," she suggested, "want to ride piggyback?" Becca sat Alvaro on a table, then carefully boosted him onto her back. "There you go! Hang on tight." Alvaro's cereal box was now clutched against *her* chest, but at least her hands were free. If grasping hold of Becca hurt, he obviously preferred pain to being without her.

Becca picked up a handful of silverware and a stack of napkins and started setting the table nearest her just as Hannah starting setting the other end. Carefully, Hannah folded a paper napkin into the kind of shape Becca had seen only at fancy restaurants like the Copper Mining Company. *Betty Crocker meets Martha Stewart*, she noted mentally before saying aloud, "You don't have to be so fussy."

Hannah raised her eyes to meet Becca's and gave a radiant smile. "Oh, I want to make it beautiful! Our pastor preached a few weeks ago on Jesus' saying, 'Whatever you do to the least of my brothers, you do to me.' " She closed her eyes for a moment as if overcome by the memory of something too beautiful for words. " '*To* me,' Jesus said. Not, '*for* me.' " She pointed to the artistically folded napkin. "So I'm setting this table for Jesus."

"That's great, Hannah," Becca said with maybe a little more sarcasm than she intended. "But I think Jesus would be more interested in having his breakfast on time than on having his napkin look pretty."

"Do you really think so?" Hannah asked, as if Becca might have some inside track on Jesus' breakfast needs. "Then I guess I'd better be faster." Her fingers flew as she continued to fold napkins, moving so quickly that she laid three place settings to Becca's four.

Becca moved to a new table, hoping Hannah would go the other direction, but Hannah moved with her, fingers flying as she continued to confide her motivation to Becca. "Did you know," she said with an enthusiasm Becca had never seen in her at school, "that Mother Teresa used to focus on that verse every time she bathed a leper's wounds?"

But Mother Teresa lived in the real world, Becca imagined herself arguing with Hannah. *She knew the poor were real people with real misery, while you don't even seem to think of the people here at all. All you're thinking of is Jesus and yourself. It's like the homeless people are just an opportunity for your own spiritual growth.*

"Mother Teresa felt that every time she touched a leper's foulness, she touched Jesus Himself," Hannah went on.

"Well, if you really want to get your hands on some foul stuff, I could arrange for you to do Jesus' laundry today," Becca told Hannah.

"Oh, could you?" Hannah breathed.

"Sure," Becca said, with a twinge of guilt. Laundry was the grossest job at the shelter. Sometimes the people who struggled with addictions or mental illness spent some of their nights on the street, especially if they were too tired or confused or drunk to make it to the shelter. And if they couldn't make it to the shelter, they usually couldn't make it to a bathroom, either. That kind of laundry had to be handled with rubber gloves. It wasn't really kind to let Hannah believe it would be some kind of holy experience, Becca admitted to herself. On the other hand, one experience washing clothes ought to put Hannah in touch with the real world.

"All right, troops! Open the doors," called Mrs. Robeson from the kitchen. "Breakfast is served."

As usual, the kids were the first through the doors. "Look, Mommy!" called out a little girl as she climbed into a chair. "My napkin looks like a crown!" She put it on her head, and her mother's tired face eased into a smile. Other kids rushed around looking for a place with one of Hannah's napkins.

"That was an awesome idea!" Nate said. "Who did that?"

Hannah looked modestly at the floor. Becca thought about keeping her mouth shut, but she knew she'd feel like a creep. "Hannah did," she said.

"Nice work," Tyler enthused, while Jacie nodded in agreement.

Nice work, Becca thought. *First you butt in on my friends, now you outshine me at the center. And to top it off, Jesus likes your napkins better than mine.*

"I have a book on origami at home," Hannah said. "I'll bring it next time and show the kids how to make something fun out of ordinary pieces of paper."

Next time—Becca began, but her thoughts were interrupted by a brisk call from Mrs. Robeson. "Servers, to the kitchen."

Becca led the way into the kitchen. She stood as far back from the sink as she could while she washed her hands, so that she wouldn't splash on Alvaro's cereal box, then picked up two plates of scrambled eggs and toast from the counter.

"Now the fun really starts," she told her friends. "It works fastest if we always come in that door—" She jerked her head to indicate the door near the sinks, and Alvaro tightened his grip around her neck "—pick up the plates here, and go out that door—" she motioned to the door at the other end of the kitchen. "That way we never run into each other and we can serve the food as fast as the cooks dish it up."

"Becca, the efficiency expert," Tyler joked.

"No point doing a thing slowly if you can do it fast!" Becca retorted.

"Don't forget the milk, Becca," Mrs. Robeson said.

"Got it, Mrs. R.," Becca replied. "Somebody can take one of these milk jugs and pour milk for whoever wants it. Be sure to ask all the kids."

"I'll do that," Hannah volunteered and headed into the dining hall with the milk.

"What about coffee?" Jacie asked. "I'd never be able to start my day without at least two cups of coffee!"

"It's on a cart in the dining hall, along with mugs and creamer and sugar," Becca explained. "People help themselves to that." She looked at the row of plates filling the counter. "Alvaro, my boy, you'll have to stay here while we serve." She carefully peeled him from around her neck and placed him on a foldaway stool in the corner. He looked at her, worry in his eyes. "You can watch us speed," she told him. He blinked. To the others she said, "Come on! Let's go."

The next half hour was a blur of activity in the kitchen as Becca, Nate, and Tyler rushed in and out. Nate and Becca made a goal of trying to whisk the plates of the serving counter as soon as the cooks filled them, and Tyler kept the cooks laughing with the outrageous compliments he paid them.

Jacie delivered her first two plates, then went over to the cart where an industrial-sized coffee pot steamed. "May I help you with that?" she said to an elderly woman shakily trying to tear open a packet of sugar. "Let me carry it back to the table for you." Taking the woman's arm, she gently steered her back to her seat, then crouched down for a few words of quiet conversation. The next time Becca passed with her hands full of plates, Jacie had unplugged the coffee pot, wrapped the cord neatly around the handle of the cart, and was pushing the cart—pot, cups, and all—

among the tables. Every time she served someone a cup, she stopped to chat a little.

Hannah was walking around the tables, too, pouring milk for the children. Becca saw one little dark-haired girl reach out a finger to touch Hannah's shiny blonde hair, and Hannah bent her head close to the girl's so she could compare the colors. Then Hannah gently stroked the girl's hair before moving on.

"Good work, crew," Mrs. Robeson finally said when everyone had been served. "Would you like to eat now?"

"You bet!" said Becca, taking a plate. "I'm starved! What about you, Alvaro?" she asked. Alvaro shook his head, gripping his cereal box tighter. "Tyler? Nate? Want to eat?"

"Sure," Tyler said. "I already had breakfast, but this looks too good to pass up." He gave a deep bow to the cooks and said, "My compliments to the chefs." Picking up a plate, he added, "I'll see if Jacie and Hannah want anything."

"Nothing for me, thanks," Nate said.

"Want to just sit and visit with some of the people, then?" Becca asked.

Nate shoved his hands in his pockets and gave an embarrassed shrug. "I'm not so good at talking with strangers." He looked so sure this was a fatal flaw that Becca felt a sudden urge to hug him. But she was conscious of Mrs. Robeson's eyes on them. "Not a problem," was all she said.

"Nate, I could use a hand with the dishwasher," Mrs. Robeson cut in. "We stack the plates on these trays, then lift them up onto the racks, and it takes a strong pair of arms. Will you help me?"

"Sure, Mrs. R.!" Nate said enthusiastically.

Becca carted Alvaro back into the dining hall. Jacie was now sitting beside a very tiny, very wrinkled old woman who had both of Jacie's hands clasped in hers. Tyler didn't seem to have had any success getting Hannah to eat with him; she was now the center of a circle of admiring little girls, their foreheads wrinkled in concentration as Hannah showed them how to fold napkins into crowns. Tyler himself was joking while he ate with a couple of men at the far table. He didn't need any help talking with strangers!

Becca ran her eye over the remaining tables until she spotted Mr. Anderson. He was a sci-fi buff, and the last time she'd volunteered at the shelter she'd lent him a copy of C. S. Lewis' *Out of the Silent Planet*. She knew he'd be eager to tell her what he thought of it, so she and Alvaro joined him at his table.

When the last person had finished eating and the dining hall was cleaned up, Mrs. Robeson gathered the workers. "How does each of you want to help out?" she asked. "If you're a people person, I can use you in one of the kids' programs. If you're not, I've got about a dozen other jobs that need doing."

"I'll do whatever is needed, Mrs. Robeson," said Hannah eagerly. "Becca suggested you might need help with the laundry."

"Did she?" Mrs. Robeson replied, shooting a piercing glance at Becca before turning back to Hannah. "I do *not* think that laundry would be the best use of your gifts, dear. I'd like to see you work with the children in the Reach Up program. That's the daycare service we provide so parents can go to our job-training clinic." She turned to Jacie. "I'd like you to go to Reach Up, too. Our senior citizens use the same room—it's good for the very young and the very old to be together—and you would be just the sunshine they need." Becca smiled. Mrs. Robeson was about the best judge of character she knew. *Everybody* said Jacie was sunshiny—but Mrs. R. had sure figured it out fast.

"What about you, Becca?" Mrs. Robeson asked. "Would you like to take these two guys to the gym and work with the basketball teams in the rec program?"

"Sure," Becca responded, "—only, I'm not sure what to do with Alvaro." The little boy was clinging to her again, piggyback-style. "He's too little to play in the gym with the big kids."

"I'll take care of Alvaro," Hannah offered. "He can play in the Reach Up room, can't he, Mrs. Robeson?"

"I don't think he'll go with you," Becca started to say, but Hannah was already reaching out for Alvaro and Alvaro was slithering down Becca's back to take Hannah's hand.

chapter 7

"Foul!" Nate yelled as a couple of 10-year-olds wrapped their arms around his knees. "We're playing basketball, not tackle football!" Grinning, he shook the kids off and took his place at the free-throw line. At 6'4", he was easily a foot taller than most of the kids in the Outreach Community Center rec program, but he still played hard enough to work up a sweat. Becca stood on the sidelines watching every move he made. She liked the way he made sure to pass the ball to every player on his team, taking a shot himself only when his team really needed the points.

Swoosh! A perfect shot. *Nice form*, Becca thought. *Very nice*.

"Becca, you go in for Tommy," one of Becca's teammates commanded. "Guard the big guy."

"You bet!" Becca called as she trotted onto the court.

"Watch out, McKinnon—I'm going left," teased Nate, feinting to his right. "Too bad you don't know left from right!"

"Are you trash-talking me, Visser?" Becca retorted. " 'Cause I can tell you right now, it's not gonna work." Nate made a fast move and Becca had to scramble to keep between him and the ball.

"Oh, yeah?" Nate moved closer to block Becca as her team got the ball. "Perfect concentration—that's what you've got?"

"Perfect," Becca agreed, taking her eyes off the ball for a second to appreciate the dimples that appeared when Nate grinned. "My mind is on only one thing."

"Uh-oh!" Nate responded. "My mother warned me about girls like you!" Now he was looking at Becca instead of the ball.

"Basketball. My mind is on basketball," she informed him, looking quickly to determine the actual location of the basketball before looking back at Nate. Eyes that blue were unusual in a guy with such dark hair.

"And I'm concentrating on making sure you don't get the basketball," Nate said, eyes locked on hers as he closed the gap between them to only a couple of inches and extended his arms to either side of her. She could feel his breath on her forehead as he leaned over her.

"Zone defense! Time for zone defense!" Tyler yelled from the sidelines. "I've seen enough man-to-woman defense!"

Nate turned to shout a wisecrack in response, and Becca quickly signaled to her teammates that she was open. Grabbing the pass, she broke past Nate and tore down the court for a solid two-pointer.

"That's game!" Tyler yelled, as Becca's team went wild. "Shake hands."

"Sorry, Nate," Becca said in her sweetest voice as her team

filed past his. "Guess you got distracted."

• • •

"That was awesome!" Tyler exclaimed at the end of the morning. His sun-bleached hair was spiky with sweat and sticking out in all directions where he had pushed it out of his eyes. He was half-sprinting on the balls of his feet, moving ahead of Becca and Nate and turning to run backward as they headed back to the shelter section of the community center. Becca could tell that he felt as pumped as she always did after a morning at the center.

"Makes you feel like some kind of superstar, the way those kids want to be near you, doesn't it?" said Nate.

"I bet a lot of them don't have good men in their lives to look up to," Tyler suggested, more soberly, and Becca suspected he was thinking about his own rocky relationship with his dad.

"Some of those older dudes looked like punks, though," Nate added. "I thought we were going to have trouble the way they were acting." He looked admiringly at Becca. "They sure treated you with respect after you whipped 'em in a little one-on-one."

"It gets their attention, anyway," she said, "and then when you want to talk about important stuff they're more ready to listen."

"My group was incredible for the Time-Out talk," Tyler said. "When you said we were breaking into small groups to talk about God in our lives, I thought you were nuts. But the guy who led my group did an awesome job. I'd like to try that sometime."

"You'd be great," Becca assured him. "It's my favorite part of the rec program." She grinned and punched Tyler in the shoulder. "See, Tyler, I *told* you you ought to be here."

"And told me, and told me," he replied. "Nagged might be a better word."

Becca shook her head. "Alyeria," she answered.

"Alyeria," Tyler agreed, touching his palm to hers.

"Yo—guys," said Nate. "Who has malaria?"

"*Alyeria*. It's a secret place we made up when we were in elementary school," Tyler explained. "Me and Becca and Solana and Jacie."

"Only somehow it got to be kind of shorthand for all sorts of things," Becca added. "Like if Solana asks me to keep a secret and I say, 'Alyeria,' she knows I'll never tell."

"So just now, it meant—?" queried Nate.

"Accountability," Becca and Tyler both answered promptly.

"We made a pact in eighth grade," Tyler explained. "To be friends forever. To want the best for each other. To encourage each other to grow in our relationships with God."

"And to nag each other if that's what it takes," Becca finished, poking a finger into Tyler's chest.

Tyler pushed open the door to the Reach Up room and went inside. Becca and Nate, following, ran into him as he stopped just inside the door, staring.

"Move it, Tyler." Becca gave him a gentle shove. "You make a better door than a . . . well, a doorway, I guess. Get out of the way."

He stepped to one side and Becca looked curiously to see what had arrested his attention. Hannah sat on the floor, looking more graceful in her long skirt than when she was standing. The little girls had apparently undone Hannah's bun and were playing with her hair clips, while Hannah's hair hung, long and shiny, like a veil half hiding her face as she bent over a little boy in her lap to point at a picture in the book she was reading him.

Jacie moved quietly from across the room and stood next to

Becca. "She looks like a Madonna, doesn't she," she murmured. "A blond one, straight out of a Pre-Raphaelite painting."

"The only blond Madonna I know is a Material Girl," Nate whispered to Becca.

"It's the light," Jacie continued, ignoring Nate and gesturing to the sunshine that streamed through the window and brought out highlights in Hannah's hair. "The light in this room is so good I've been sketching half the morning," she made a face, "with a broken crayon from the toy box. I'm getting lots of ideas for the homecoming window."

The little boy on Hannah's lap turned his head toward them. "Becca!" he cried, and hurried over to grasp Becca's shirttail. Becca hoped she didn't look as startled as she felt. She had forgotten all about Alvaro once she'd fallen into the routine of the rec program. She might have gone home without him—and it would be hard to explain to her parents why she had left Alvaro at the homeless shelter!

"Oh, Becca," Hannah said, getting up awkwardly from the floor, "Alvaro is just like you, isn't he?"

"I doubt it," Becca answered. She couldn't think of anything she and Alvaro had in common—certainly not the desire to sit quietly, much less on Hannah's lap!

"He is simply the most tenacious child I've ever met," Hannah went on, in what Becca was beginning to think of as her textbook voice. "Like you."

"Oh," said Tyler, "you mean stubborn!" He winced as Becca elbowed him in the ribs.

"That cereal box of his," Hannah said indulgently. "When he wants something, he hangs on to it with all he's got. But," she added brightly, "he's learning to let go a little and share, aren't you

Alvaro?" At this, both Tyler and Jacie elbowed Becca.

"That's a really good lesson, don't you think, Becca?" Jacie said, with a look that let Becca know that, while Hannah might be talking about hanging onto cereal, Jacie was talking about bigger issues.

"Alyeria," Tyler breathed in Becca's ear before helping Hannah pack her children's books in her bag.

"Morning shift is over, team," Mrs. Robeson announced, coming into the room with a clipboard under her arm. "Thank you all for coming today." She glanced over the notes on her clipboard, nodded crisply, and looked back up. "I'm pleased with the work you did today. Each of you made a real contribution."

"How does she know that?" Nate whispered to Becca.

"Mrs. R. sees *everything*," Becca whispered back.

"I would be happy to have any of you volunteer again," Mrs. Robeson continued. "Becca can let you know what her volunteer schedule is—"

"Don't worry, Mrs. R.," Tyler put in. "She already does that. She's positively *tenacious* about it. You could almost call it nagging." He flashed Becca a mischievous grin.

"—or you can call my office and set up your own times to come in if you're interested," Mrs. Robeson finished. "Again, thank you for your help today," she added, then walked briskly away.

"Lunch?" said Tyler as soon as Mrs. Robeson was gone.

"Definitely," Becca said. "I've even got money today. My mom gave me cash to make sure Alvaro gets something to eat." As if on cue, Alvaro reached into his cereal box for a handful of Lucky Charms.

"I'm in," said Jacie. "How about you, Nate? Hannah?"

"Sounds good," Nate agreed, and Hannah nodded.

"Where should we go?" Becca asked as they walked to the parking lot.

"Crazy Charlie's?" Tyler suggested.

"Isn't that the place with the video arcade?" asked Hannah hesitantly.

"Yeah," Tyler said. "And bowling and laser tag and stuff. You mean you've never been there?"

Hannah shuddered. "Oh, no. I don't think I'd care for the kind of people who go there at all."

"*We* go there," Becca pointed out. "And we're not exactly juvenile delinquents."

Hannah just shook her head.

"We can go somewhere else," Jacie said. "The food's not so hot at Crazy Charlie's anyway, and I don't have time to hang out after lunch. I have to be at work at two. What about that new pie place—Mimi's?"

"Where the old Denny's used to be?" Nate asked.

"Yeah. I heard it's pretty good," Jacie said. "Okay with you guys?"

Becca shrugged. She didn't want to spend the afternoon at Crazy Charlie's either, but it bugged her the way Hannah seemed to have veto power over their plans. *Deal with it,* she told herself. *At least the rest of us are doing something together.*

"I'll ride with you, Becca, so you don't get lost," Nate said. "Besides, your front seat has a lot more leg room than Jacie's backseat!" He opened the driver's door for Becca, then helped Alvaro onto his booster seat in the back. Tyler made a face as he squeezed into the back of Jacie's car.

"What do you think of the center?" Becca asked as they pulled out of the parking lot. Now that she had decided not to let Hannah bother her—for now—she felt the familiar high she always got from working at the center, and she was eager to share it with Nate. But Nate didn't answer right away, and Becca felt some of her exhilaration drain away. "You hated it, didn't you?" she finally said, thinking of how uncomfortable Nate had been about talking with the people in the homeless shelter.

"No." Something in Nate's voice made Becca look over at him. His thick eyebrows were drawn together in a frown of concentration. "No," he said again, with more conviction. "I didn't hate it. But I felt like . . . like I was going somewhere I'd never been. Not just that I hadn't been to the Outreach Community Center building. It was like I was walking into a whole new country." He flashed Becca a self-conscious smile. "I mean, that way of living your faith—that's new to me."

"What do you mean?" Becca prompted.

"Well, I'm a Christian. At least, I go to church, and I really do believe in Jesus. But I guess I never thought *living* like a Christian meant much more than not doing the 'big' sins. I figured I was living my faith because I don't cheat on tests, and I don't sleep around, and I don't drink or do drugs—you know."

"Uh-huh," Becca agreed.

"But at the center it's like I got this picture of how much bigger the Christian life could be." He glanced over at Becca. "Does that sound cheesy?"

"No!" Becca answered quickly. "I feel the same way."

"I feel like there might be this whole way of living that isn't just about me and what I want. Like I have something to give—and I want to give it." Nate shook his head. "That sounds arrogant, doesn't it?"

Becca shook her head. "No, it sounds like what I want, too. I want to count for something more than just having fun and getting good grades or whatever."

"You're an amazing girl, Becca. I never talk like this to anyone," Nate said.

"I'm not that amazing," Becca said ruefully. "Solana says I only want to live my faith when it's convenient to me."

"Well," Nate said, "you're amazing to me."

chapter 8

Becca knew she had a dopey smile on her face as she, Nate, and Alvaro walked into Mimi's, but she didn't care. She even gave Hannah one of her friendliest smiles. Nate thought she was amazing—well, maybe she could amaze herself.

"Wow, they've really changed this place since it was a Denny's," said Tyler as they waited to be seated. "Look—they've flipped everything around so it's like a mirror image of the old restaurant."

"You're right," Nate said. "The salad bar used to be on that side; now it's on this side."

"Why do they do that?" Becca asked. "It just confuses people."

"Trying to make it feel new, I guess," Tyler suggested. "Most people don't confuse as easily as you!"

As soon as they were squeezed into a booth, Jacie announced, "I have to use the restroom."

Becca felt Jacie's foot pressing down on hers under the table. "I'll go with you," she said at once. "Hannah, will you keep Alvaro from following me?"

"Why do girls always go to the restroom in groups?" Tyler complained as Becca and Jacie hurried from the table.

"That was smart, asking Hannah to watch Alvaro," Jacie said as soon as they were in the restroom. "I didn't want her to come, but I couldn't exactly say so."

"Why are we in here?" Becca giggled as Jacie looked under the doors of the stalls to make sure they were alone.

"What happened on the way over?" Jacie demanded. "When you got out of the car you were all lit up like you had a fireworks show going on inside you. What gives? Did Nate kiss you?"

"No! Jacie, give me a break! We haven't even gone out yet," Becca exclaimed. "You know I don't give kisses away that easily." She dropped her voice to a confidential whisper. "Not that I didn't think about it this morning while we were playing basketball."

"Basketball!" Jacie protested. "I can't think of anything less romantic!"

"Depends on how you play it," Becca retorted, and both girls burst into a fit of giggles.

"Shh! Somebody will hear us!" Jacie said, sucking in her cheeks to make herself stop laughing. "So if he didn't kiss you, what did happen in the car? I know something did."

Becca stopped giggling and pressed her fist to her mouth, still smiling. "I don't know, exactly," she said at last. "We just had such a good conversation—no, really!" she insisted when Jacie rolled her eyes. "He was talking about his faith, and the ideas he has about what kind of a Christian he wants to be. It was the kind of conversation you always want to have with a guy but hardly ever do, you know? Except with Tyler," she added as an afterthought, "but he's not a real guy."

Jacie gave a little snort that set them off in giggles again. "I don't think Tyler would appreciate that comment!"

"You know what I mean. You couldn't imagine ever kissing Tyler," Becca said.

Jacie just raised her eyebrows.

"Jacie! You couldn't! That would be . . . that would be like kissing your own brother!" Becca insisted.

"Anyway," Jacie said, "you *can* imagine kissing Nate, so I think it's very cool that there's more to him than meets the eye."

"Although what meets the eye is very nice," Becca pointed out.

"Sure," Jacie said, "if you like 'em tall, dark, and handsome."

"With dimples and a great smile," Becca added.

"And the kind of cheekbones you see on male models," Jacie said.

"And blue eyes that turn your stomach to Jell-O when they look into yours," Becca confided.

"And broad shoulders."

"And great moves on the court."

"Honey, you've got it bad," said Jacie, and both girls dissolved into giggles again.

"Get it together, girls," Becca said to their reflections in the mirror. "You are not a couple of airheaded, boy-crazy females. You are intelligent girls capable of acting appropriately around the opposite sex."

Jacie nodded approvingly. "Amen, sister!"

"Think we ought to go back now?" Becca said. "I bet Hannah's never been alone with two guys this long in her life."

Jacie led the way back to their table. Just before they got there, Becca grabbed her arm. "Jacie! We forgot to *use* the restroom! And now I really have to go!"

"Hold it!" Jacie hissed, and slid into the booth beside Hannah, leaving the space next to Nate for Becca.

All through lunch Becca felt as if little bubbles of happiness were fizzing inside her. Mostly they talked about the community center. Every time Nate's leg brushed against hers under the table she felt a little shiver run through her. Jacie kept catching her eye, then looking away quickly so they wouldn't burst into giggles again. Alvaro ate his way steadily through the kid's meal Becca ordered for him, and even Hannah seemed to be talking like a normal person—maybe because she had a hard time getting a word in edgewise.

Suddenly Jacie exclaimed, "I almost forgot! I have to be to work at two!" She looked at her watch. "I'm gonna have to go in a couple minutes."

"Me too," said Becca. "I want to do some paragliding this afternoon."

"That looks like an awesome sport," Nate said. "Is it as fun as it looks?"

"Better," Becca said emphatically.

"Do you really jump out of an airplane?" Hannah asked. She looked horrified.

"No, that's para*chuting*. I go para*gliding*. It's like a combination of parachuting and hang gliding," Becca explained. "You start from the ground, and you soar, like in hang gliding, but you use different equipment. A hang glider is kind of like a big kite you ride, right?" she said. She decided not to assume Hannah knew anything about extreme sports. "In paragliding you use a chute, but it's not round like the kind sky divers use. A paragliding chute is more oblong, and it has lots of little channels that fill up with air to give it shape." She looked at her friends' faces. "I'm losing you, aren't I? Okay—picture a giant eyebrow in the sky. That's the shape of the chute. I'm attached to a harness about 35 feet below the chute."

Jacie shuddered. "It sounds awful—hanging up there in the air like that."

"It probably would be awful for you, Jacie, with your fear of heights," Becca agreed, "but for me it's one of the most free feelings I've ever had. And it's not like I'm hanging by my armpits or anything—the whole harness is more like a seat. Oh, I can't even begin to explain it. You have to try it to believe it."

"Faith is like that, too," Hannah said. "You have to try it to believe it."

There was a little silence at this abrupt change of subject, then Becca said, "Okay . . . well, excuse me for a minute, will you?"

"Are you going to the . . . ladies' room?" Hannah asked hesitantly. "I'll go with you."

"Again?" Tyler said to Becca.

"Too much Mountain Dew, I guess—not that it's any of your business," Becca said, while Jacie made a strangled sound and quickly took a swallow of water. "Keep an eye on Alvaro for me?"

Hannah was blushing a deep crimson, and Becca guessed she was embarrassed to mention the restroom in mixed company. Becca quickly led the way to the restrooms, and Hannah followed, head down. *Not quite like my trip with Jacie*, Becca thought as they entered the stalls in silence.

A few seconds later Becca heard the restroom door open again.

Then she heard male voices. *What are men doing in the women's restroom?* she thought indignantly. She was just about to yell through the stall door for the men to leave when an unwelcome thought occurred to her. Had she chosen the door on the left or the right?

Oh, no! she realized. *I'm in the men's restroom!*

Quickly she looked down at her legs, trying to estimate how much the men could see if they happened to look at the stall door. Basketball shoes and athletic socks—pretty gender-generic. But what about Hannah? Cautiously, Becca ducked her head to look at the stall next to hers. No sign of Hannah. *She must have pulled her legs up to hide them*, Becca thought.

Suddenly Becca felt a fit of giggles coming on. The more she tried to squelch them, the more hysterically funny the situation seemed. *Trapped in the men's restroom! What if more guys come in before these men leave? We could be hiding in the stalls till closing time!* Just when Becca thought she would burst from holding in her laughter, the main door opened again and she heard the men leave. Becca waited a few seconds, listening, then cautiously opened the door to her stall.

"You can come out, Hannah! The coast is clear," she managed to choke out before she dissolved into laughter. She stopped abruptly at the sight of Hannah's tear-streaked face. "Oh, Hannah," she began, "it's okay—"

"This is not funny, Becca," Hannah hissed. "This was a mean trick!"

"A trick? You think I did this on purpose?" Becca was stupefied. "Hannah, it was a mistake."

Hannah swept past Becca and stalked through the restaurant to their booth. "You've never liked me," she said over her shoulder to Becca, "but you didn't have to go out of your way to humiliate me." She turned to Jacie. "Will you take me home now, please?"

Jacie looked from Hannah to Becca. "What on earth happened?"

Hannah crossed her arms and pressed her lips tightly shut.

"It was a mistake," Becca said. "We went in the men's restroom by mistake."

"That's it?" Nate looked at Hannah, who was now quivering as if she were holding back tears or rage—or both. "That doesn't seem like such a big deal."

"It's obviously a big deal to Hannah," Tyler said gently, reaching across Jacie to put his hand on Hannah's arm. Hannah pulled away and Tyler turned to Becca. "What did you go and pull a stunt like that for, Becca?" he demanded angrily.

"I told you," Becca said. "It was a mistake."

Alvaro's big eyes moved to follow the conversation. He said nothing, his empty fork halfway between the plate and his mouth.

"A mistake? Becca, you just went in the restroom half an hour ago with Jacie. How could it be a mistake?"

"I wasn't paying attention, I guess," Becca said lamely. "And they must have switched the restrooms around like they did the salad bar and everything else in this place. Last time I was here, the women's room was on the right."

"Well, they didn't change them in the last half hour," Tyler pointed out.

"Cut her some slack, man," Nate said. "We all know she can't tell left from right. So she went in the wrong door. Did anybody die?"

To Becca it felt like something *had* died as they paid the bill and walked out in silence, Alvaro clinging to her hand. All the fun had gone out of the day. She tried again to apologize to Hannah, but Hannah bit her lip and shook her head, looking away. Maybe Tyler seemed to think Hannah was being noble by not yelling at Becca, but Becca wished she'd say something—anything.

It didn't help when Jacie pulled her aside. "Becca, don't worry about it. Sometimes a joke goes wrong. I know you didn't mean anything by it."

Becca didn't know whether to explode or cry. "Jacie," she finally said, "I don't lie to you. I never lie to you. It wasn't a joke; it was an accident."

"You're right, Becca—I should have believed you right away," Jacie said immediately. "I'm sorry!"

"Okay," said Becca. But it still hurt to know that at first Jacie believed Hannah's side of the story over hers.

In the parking lot, Hannah got into Jacie's car. "Coming?" Tyler asked Nate as Becca buckled Alvaro into his booster seat.

"No, thanks," Nate said. "I'll catch a ride with Becca if she'll take me." He added in an undertone to Becca, "Unless you'd rather be alone?"

"No, climb in," Becca said, closing the rear door. "I'm glad one friend hasn't abandoned me."

"Two," Nate corrected. "Don't forget old Alvaro here." Becca gave him a weak smile.

They drove in silence for awhile, except for the directions Nate gave, since Becca didn't know where he lived. It was a comfortable silence though. After awhile, Nate said, "Tyler's not mad at you, you know."

"Coulda fooled me," Becca said.

"Nah. He's mad because Hannah's upset and he can't fix it."

Nate reached over as if to touch Becca's cheek. His glance fell into the backseat at Alvaro and withdrew his hand. "We guys are like that. If we care about a girl, we want to take care of her."

"Did it ever occur to you that maybe a girl can take care of herself?" Becca asked.

"Absolutely," Nate said. His voice took on a teasing tone. "Some girls can even whip us in a game of basketball. Thing is, we still want to fix things for them when they get hurt. And when we can't, we get mad. Like Tyler is right now."

They rode in silence a little longer. The only sounds came from the backseat—an occasional crinkling of paper, and the sound of gentle munching.

I know what Nate means, Becca decided. *I'm a fixer, too. When something's wrong, I don't want to sit around and see what happens; I want to* do *something*. Without realizing it, she pressed the accelerator harder. *Even if it doesn't solve the problem, I've gotta do something.*

"Hang on, Alvaro!" Nate called over the seat. "Becca thinks she's driving a jet!"

"Great idea!" she said.

"No, no, bad idea," Nate exclaimed, pressing his hands against the dashboard. "We're too young to die!"

"Oh, sorry," Becca said, glancing at the speedometer and lifting her foot from the gas. "I didn't mean speeding was a good idea. I meant flying was a good idea. After I drop you off, I'm going gliding."

chapter 

J O U R N A L

Saturday, October 13

Sometimes I just don't understand what God is thinking.

Take last Saturday. Everything was going so well! Okay, I guess I could have been nicer to Hannah at the center, and Alvaro was kind of a pain with his clinging. But then Nate and I had a great talk in the car and everybody was having a good time at Mimi's. It seemed like my group of friends was back to normal. Even Hannah didn't seem to be doing her "look at me—I'm the new girl" act. For once I wasn't wishing she'd leave us alone. I was even thinking it wouldn't be so bad if she kept hanging out with us. All we needed was Solana to make it perfect.

And then Hannah freaked out in the bathroom.

That's what I don't get. I was trying to be nice to Hannah. Isn't that what God wanted me to do? So why did He let it all turn out so awful?

It's so stupid. It was a dumb mistake and it should be over. But it's been a week and things still aren't really normal. Everything is weird—and a little strained. Hannah talks to me, but only when she absolutely has to. I'm not sure I really want to talk to her, either. Tyler says Hannah's not sure she can trust me. She should talk! Who went sneaking around Jacie's back to place her private painting in a public show? Hannah. Who twisted the facts of the bathroom incident to make me look like the bad guy? Hannah.

What makes it so unfair is that it all started because I was trying to do what God would want and be nice to

HANNAH. IF I HADN'T GONE WITH HER TO THE RESTROOM . . . OR IF I HADN'T TRIED TO HURRY SO SHE WOULDN'T FEEL EMBARRASSED . . .

Becca sighed and closed the spiral notebook she was writing in. *If Hannah had never invaded our group, none of this would have happened.*

"Becca," Mrs. McKinnon called as she knocked on the door, "may I come in?"

Becca opened her bedroom door for her mom, who walked in with a basket of clean laundry on her hip. She put the laundry basket on the floor and sat down on the bed.

"I found this in your shorts pocket," she said, handing Becca a folded sheet of notebook paper. Becca opened it and read the first few lines:

T MINUS 21 DAYS AND COUNTING. ONLY THREE MORE WEEKS OF ALVARO.

The page she'd written in algebra class! She'd forgotten it was in her pocket when she threw those shorts in the laundry. Quickly she folded it back up.

"Did you read it?" she asked her mom.

"Of course not!" her mom answered. "You know I wouldn't read anything that might be private." She shifted her weight on the bed. "Why? Is it something I should know about?"

"No. Yes. I don't know," said Becca. "I don't know anything anymore."

"Hmmm. Want to go for a walk?" her mom asked.

Becca nodded. She and her mom had their best talks when

they walked. And no matter how busy her mom got, she almost always seemed to know when Becca really needed to talk.

"So . . ." said her mom once they were on the trail in the undeveloped property behind their backyard, then fell silent. That was her standard opening line anytime Becca had something serious to discuss, and Becca loved her for it. She knew her mom would never push her to talk or try to pry information out of her, like some parents who seemed to think family conversation ranked right up there with the Spanish Inquisition.

"My friends came to the community center last Saturday," Becca said.

"Yes, I know," her mother replied. "Mrs. Robeson told me. She was pleased to get a new volunteer."

"What do you mean?" Becca asked.

"Hannah Connor," her mother said. "She's working with the after-school program now—didn't you know?"

"No, I didn't," Becca said, unconsciously speeding up her pace. "You mean, she's there regularly?"

"She was there Monday, Wednesday, and Friday this week."

"I don't believe it!"

Hesitantly at first, then eager to get it all out, Becca told her mother about the fancy napkins, the kids clustering around Hannah, and how Mrs. Robeson talked about Hannah's gifts. "And now Mrs. R. will probably want Hannah all the time instead of me. She probably didn't even notice what I was doing because I was off in the gym with Tyler and Nate."

Mrs. McKinnon put a hand on Becca's arm. "Can we slow down? We're practically running!" After a couple of deep breaths, she said, "Becca, I'm very proud of you for the faithfulness you've shown in your commitment to the community center. You've volunteered at least once a month for—what?—three years now? Trust me, Mrs. Robeson isn't going to forget about you." Now *she* started walking faster. "So—tell me about this Nate."

"Well, he's cute," Becca started, "but as you know," she gave her mother a sly smile, "it's character that counts."

"You've got that right," said her mother. "So . . ."

Becca described the way Nate interacted with the kids at the center. "He's a Christian—you know I'm not interested in going out with anybody who isn't. Not that he's exactly asked me out," she added ruefully.

"Hmm," said her mother.

"He's one of Tyler's friends from the basketball team," Becca explained, "and I thought we were all going to go to homecoming together, but that fell through." She wasn't sure who her mom would sympathize with—her or Hannah—but one of the unwritten rules of their walks was that her mom never lectured, even on a subject she might have a lot to say about if they discussed it, say, at the supper table. It was as if she went into unconditional listening mode for as long as they were on the trail. So Becca described the way the group homecoming date had transpired and expired, and her ongoing frustrations with Hannah.

"Well," her mom said, "it sounds as if you're feeling like everything's uncertain with Nate, and uncertain with your friends, and uncertain at the community center. And on top of it all, your dad and I ask you to think about adding Alvaro to our family. You must feel like the ground is sliding right out from beneath your feet."

"You got that right," Becca said.

They walked a little way without speaking. Slowly, Becca started to relax. Sometimes she thought walking in the woods was like spending time in another world. She loved the way the light filtered through the leaves in the summer, and the way the light and shadow flickered when the aspen leaves quaked.

This time of the year, a walk on this trail could be like walking in a leaf snowstorm, as the leaves fluttered lazily but persistently to the ground. Becca loved to scuff up big piles of leaves while the ground rustled with the sound of squirrels and chipmunks scurrying to bury the last of the nuts before winter.

Something was nagging at the edges of Becca's mind—something she wanted to ask her mom. What was it? Something she'd thought of while she was talking and tucked away to come back to. Almost without thinking, she turned around and headed back down the trail, as if to mentally retrace the conversation. Hannah. Nate. The community center.

The community center. That was it.

"Mom," she said, "you really love the community center."

"Mmm-hmm," her mom agreed.

"I mean, you *really* love the community center. You love it enough that you made all kinds of changes in our family life so you could work there."

"Yes, I suppose I did have to make some changes when I went back to work," said her mom. "You can understand that now that it's such a big part of your life, can't you?"

"Yeah, I can," Becca said. "But what I can't understand is why you said you would take a leave of absence if you had to. If we, you know, adopt Alvaro."

"That seems strange to you," her mom said.

"It *is* strange," Becca responded. "Why would you give up the community center, even for a little while?"

"Let me ask you this," her mom answered. "What is it about

the community center that you love so much?"

Becca thought a moment. "I guess," she said slowly, "what I love most is that it's a safe place. A haven. Homeless people can find a place there. Kids who might get in trouble on the street can come in to play basketball and learn about Jesus. Kids who get put down in school find tutors who won't laugh at their mistakes."

"You think that's important? To feel safe? Do you think that tells people something about God?" her mom asked.

"Yeah, I do," Becca said. "I think . . ." she paused to find just the right words. "I think God is the ultimate Safe Place. Even though I don't feel like He's so safe for me right now," she admitted.

"Oh?"

"Not really. I feel more like He's taking away the things that make me feel safe," Becca answered.

"You're losing the things that make you feel secure," her mom said.

"Exactly! Like my best friends are out of whack and—" Becca paused. She didn't really want to tell her mom that she didn't feel secure in their family any more. "And stuff," she finished lamely.

"People are what make you feel secure."

"Yeah," Becca said. "I know it's God, ultimately, but He does it through people too. Do you know what I mean?"

"I do," her mom nodded. "Is that what the community center does, do you think?"

"It does," Becca said. "Think about that fabric sculpture in the lobby. We were looking at it last Saturday and talking about all the things it reminded us of. I didn't think of it then, but it wouldn't be the same if it were just Jesus with one person. It's like the more you have people who care about you, the more you can feel God's arms around you."

"I love that idea, Becca!" exclaimed her mom, with a note of such exuberance that Becca stopped looking at the light and shadows and instead looked at her mom as she strode along the trail. *She looks young*, Becca realized. *Young and strong and like she's looking ahead.*

"So . . ." Becca said.

"So," finished her mom, "that's what I love about the community center, too. Being a small part of creating a safe place for people. Being one of the people who cares."

"Okay," said Becca patiently, "but why would you want to give that up?"

"Becca," her mom said in surprise, "don't you know that it works both ways? The more you have people who care about you, the more you can feel God's arms around you. And the more people *you* care for, the more you feel God's arms around you. If we adopt Alvaro, I won't be giving up what I love about the center. I'll just be bringing it closer to home!"

"But wouldn't that be like working all the time and never having a break?" Becca asked.

"Oh, Honey!" Becca's mom gave her a hug. "I'm not looking to take a break from doing what God wants me to do! Are you?"

I know the right *answer to that question*, Becca thought, *but I don't know if it's* my *answer.*

chapter 10

"Class dismissed."

Becca grabbed her algebra book and spiral notebook and hurried to the hall. She counted five lockers to the right of the classroom door—and stopped. Nate was turning the combination lock.

"No way!" said Becca, looking up and then down the hall. "I did not go the wrong direction this time!" She grabbed the neck of Nate's T-shirt like a cop collaring a suspect. "Visser—you're messing with my mind. This is my locker, not yours."

"Busted!" Nate said, turning his attention from the lock and straightening up. Becca kept her grip on his shirt as he stood and turned to face her. *If I put my other hand behind his neck*, she thought, *we could be slow dancing. Or kissing.* Of course, she couldn't with her algebra books under one arm. Of course she wouldn't right here in the hall.

With the deftness that made him a champion ball-stealer on the basketball court, Nate slipped Becca's books out from under her arm and held them above his head with both hands. "I've got possession," he said.

"Grow up, Visser," Becca said, with a smile that let Nate know she didn't really mean it.

"Speak for yourself, shorty," Nate said as Becca stood on tiptoes and reached for her books. His face was close to hers now, and Becca decided Jacie was right—he did have great cheekbones.

"That does it," Becca said. "Nobody makes fun of my height!" She made a lunge for her books, pinning Nate against the lockers and throwing them both off balance.

"Personal foul!" he called as he brought one arm around Becca's waist to steady her. Becca was intensely aware of how muscular his chest and arms were in the brief moment their bodies were pressed together. Quickly, she pulled back. For just a second, Nate's arm tightened around her, then he let go. Suddenly, he didn't seem to know what to do with his hands. While he was still off guard, Becca seized her books and gave a small shout of triumph.

"Don't you ever give up?" said Nate.

"Nope." Becca shook her head decidedly. "Not when it's so much fun to beat you," she added with a grin.

"So, who do you think will win the homecoming game?" Nate asked. He seemed to be having trouble with his hands again. He put them in his pockets, then pulled them out, then crossed his arms.

He's nervous, Becca realized. *He wants to talk about homecoming and he's nervous. That is so cute.*

"The Studs," she told him. "Who else? You ought to know—you're a Stud yourself."

"Technically not till basketball season," Nate said.

"Oh, I wouldn't say that," Becca answered, raising an eyebrow.

Nate opened his mouth. Closed it. Then he said, "What were we talking about?"

"Homecoming," Becca said innocently.

Nate put his hands back in his pockets. "Oh, yeah. So it looks like this group thing isn't going to work out, huh?"

"Looks like it," Becca agreed.

"I was hoping it would," Nate said, taking his hands out of his pockets and crossing his arms again.

"Me, too," said Becca.

"So, are you having a party at your house instead?" he asked.

"No." Becca shook her head.

"Um, do you have other plans?" he asked.

"Not yet." Becca smiled.

Nate uncrossed his arms again. "Want to go together?" he finally asked.

"Sure," said Becca. *I've only been waiting two weeks for you to ask me!* "I'd like that. You'll have to meet my parents first, though. That's one of their rules to make sure I don't go out with ax murderers or drug dealers."

"That's cool," said Nate. "I'll leave my ax in the trunk." He put his hands back in his pockets, but now the gesture looked relaxed. He was whistling as he walked away.

● ● ●

"Hi, Maggie," Becca called to the wiry little woman behind the counter of the community center's resale shop. "A Doberman personality in a Chihuahua body" was how her dad always described Maggie. "How's business?" Becca asked.

"Pretty good. We got three cartons of dishes from Heritage Baptist Church this week. I think they're redoing their church kitchen. Ugly as sin, their dishes."

Becca wandered over to the housewares aisle. Maggie was right; those were ugly dishes. But on one of the shelves she saw a yellow plastic bowl with a hinged lid. It was shaped like a Cheerio and had the Cheerios logo on it. It looked like something you could get by sending in box tops.

"Alvaro, look at this," she said to the little boy clutching the hammer loop on her utility jeans. "See," she said, showing him how the lid snapped open and shut. "You could put your Cheerios in this. Then you wouldn't need to carry a box." She turned it over to look at the price. "Fifty cents. Want me to buy it for you?"

Alvaro looked from the bowl to his cereal box—Cheerios again, since Mrs. McKinnon had gone to the grocery store. He let go of Becca's jeans to try the lid. He couldn't work it with only one hand, so he carefully set his Cheerios box on the floor and took the bowl from Becca.

"You like it?" she asked. "It's yours." She walked over to the cash register and handed Maggie a dollar bill.

"Looking for anything special today?" Maggie asked as she gave Becca her change.

"Yeah." Becca grinned. "A homecoming dress."

"Are you crazy?" Maggie said. "You're going to buy your homecoming dress at the resale shop? Why don't you go someplace nice?"

"I like secondhand clothes," Becca said. "They've got character. And after all, it's character that counts." She laughed and Maggie looked at her questioningly. "Family joke," Becca explained.

"When is your homecoming?" Maggie asked.

"Next Saturday."

"*Next* Saturday?" Maggie said. "Not exactly planning ahead, are you?"

"I had to wait for the Lakeview shipment to come in, didn't I?" said Becca. The resale shop always got a lot of formals right after Lakeview High's homecoming, which fortunately was the week before Stony Brook's. "Lucky for me that no one wants to wear the same homecoming dress twice," she added.

With a glance to see that Alvaro was still happily occupied, Becca went over to the clothing racks. She felt buoyant, with the same sense of anticipation she had when she went paragliding, in the moment when her chute filled with air just before her feet left the ground.

I suppose I ought to be ashamed of myself for getting so worked up over a guy, she told herself. But she wasn't. *And now I understand how Jacie got so swept away by Damien.*

She let her thoughts drift into snapshots of her limited times with Nate. Nate was fun, and he was cute, and he seemed to think she was pretty terrific. *Which doesn't seem to be the opinion of a lot of people lately*, she reminded herself. But right now that didn't bother her. She felt bighearted enough to forget the tensions Hannah's misunderstanding caused between her and her friends. She even felt fonder of Alvaro than she had since the family council.

With the speed that came from much practice, Becca flipped through the hangers on the racks. She could tell pretty fast which clothes were in good shape and which were shabby, which were interestingly quirky and which were just plain bizarre. She didn't bother to look at the size. At the resale shop, half the tags were cut out anyway, by the first owners who presumably found them too scratchy.

In a few minutes, Becca had gathered an armload of dresses. She carried her choices into the curtained alcove that served as a dressing room and started to try them on. First, a flashy red strapless number that she knew she would never wear, but just looked fun. She zipped it up, and the bodice immediately drooped to her waist. Becca laughed at her half-naked reflection. She'd never have a bustline big enough to keep this dress up! Jacie, now—she'd hold it up beautifully. Sometimes Becca was jealous of Jacie's curves. *But*, she rationalized, *think what a pain it would be on the basketball court. I'd need a sports bra made of steel to keep down the bounce.*

Last year she and Jacie and Solana had spent the afternoon together before homecoming, and Jacie did their hair. When the other girls saw the results, Jacie was in big demand. Becca wondered whether she'd be busy doing hair this year or if she'd just hang out somewhere with Hannah. She decided she didn't really want to know.

Here's a Solana dress, she thought as she pulled a black spandex dress off the hanger and slipped it over her head. It took a lot of twisting and adjusting to get the seams lined up in all the right places. Becca examined herself in the mirror. The skin-tight dress left little to the imagination. *Definitely a Solana dress*, Becca decided. She turned sideways to assess her figure. *You look like a jock*, she told her reflection. *Tight butt, flat stomach—that's good. Flat chest—can't do anything about that. Arms and legs more strong-looking than sexy*. Becca gave a nod to the girl in the mirror. Given the choice between a body that *looked* great and a body that *worked* great, she thought she'd choose function over form. She smiled, remembering playing basketball with Nate. You didn't have to look like a model to get close to a guy.

With some difficulty, she peeled off the outfit. Even if she wanted to wear something that revealing, her father would probably veto it. He wasn't authoritarian about much, but he did get serious about what signals his girls were sending with their clothes. Anyway, even if she wanted it she'd probably never even get this dress out of the store. She could just imagine what Maggie would say if she brought a spandex dress to the cash register.

Becca picked up a dress in a funky shade of blue, somewhere between aqua and teal. It caught her eye on the rack because it was just the color of the house her dad had stayed in on his last missions trip to Honduras. Once she saw the picture of the house, Becca noticed the same shade of blue in lots of her dad's photographs—from plastic chairs to shutters. Mentally, she'd named that color Honduras blue. She always meant to see if Jacie had a tube to match it in her acrylic paints, but she kept forgetting.

The Honduras blue dress slid easily over Becca's head. It had wide straps and a square neck and about thirty tiny buttons down the back. Becca noticed with delight that the buttons were carved with an intricate design. She fastened all the ones she could reach, then stuck her head past the curtain to call for Maggie. "Can you leave the counter for a minute to help me?"

"Sure," Maggie answered. "Find anything you like?"

"What do you think of this one?" Becca asked as Maggie swiftly did up the remaining buttons. The dress hung trim but not tight. The front was simple, but the back looked pretty special with the buttons and deep V cut that was echoed by a set-in V waist. Becca pulled the scrunchie from her ponytail and let her hair fall loose. It swung just below her shoulders.

"You could wear your hair down with this and still not cover up the detailing in the back," Maggie observed. "You planning to wear it up or down?"

"Down, I think," said Becca. She didn't think she could very well ask Jacie to do her hair when she knew Jacie wanted her to stay home and host the gang. Besides, Nate seemed to like it down.

"I'd lose the dog tags," Maggie said, pointing to the three chains around Becca's neck.

"I guess," Becca laughed. "My mom has some great South American jewelry that I bet has just this shade of blue in it. She has some parrot earrings, I think, and there's probably a necklace that could go with them."

"That would be different," Maggie observed. "Make a nice change from pearls, I suppose."

Becca laughed. "I'm not a pearls kind of girl, Maggie. If I'm going to wear pearls, I want to dive for them myself." She spun in front of the mirror. "I think I'll get this."

"It does look nice on you," Maggie said approvingly. "You carry it off with a kind of flair, if you know what I mean." She looked at the hem. "It's long on you, though. You'll have to wear heels. I hope your date isn't short."

"Oh, no, he's not short," Becca assured her. "Heels won't be a problem." She rose up on tiptoe to see how the dress hung, and felt an odd thrill in her stomach remembering how it was to lean against Nate on tiptoe in the hall. "Help me out of this, will you, Maggie?" she said. "This is the dress for me."

Maggie undid the buttons, then went back to her post at the counter. Becca was pulling her T-shirt over her head when she heard an outraged yell from Maggie.

"Becca!" Maggie hollered. She sounded really mad. "Get out here now!"

chapter 11

Becca yanked her shirt down and fumbled with the fitting room curtain. She ran out in her bare feet, wondering what made Maggie holler like that. Shoplifters, maybe? Nobody dangerous—Maggie sounded angry, not scared.

She rushed into the shop area and stopped short. Maggie stood in the housewares aisle, hands on her hips and face flushed, but Becca couldn't see what she was so mad about.

Then she looked down. *Oh*.

Actually, lots of O's. Alvaro sat on the floor in a galaxy of scattered Cheerios. Looking up at her, he picked up his cereal box and poured some Cheerios in his bowl. More landed on the floor than in the bowl.

"I'm sorry, Maggie," Becca said. "I'll clean it up."

"I'll say you will!" Maggie retorted, with more annoyance than Becca thought the situation called for. Becca took a step toward Alvaro and stopped as she heard a *crunch* and felt an unpleasant sensation underfoot.

"Yuck!" she said, as she examined the powdered cereal sticking to her bare foot.

"Yuck is right," said Maggie. "Look." She pointed angrily around the store, and Becca realized that Cheerios trails led up and down nearly every aisle—some already crushed into the carpet as if Alvaro had walked in them himself.

"Wow," she said, looking at the thousands of little O's. "It must have been a new box."

"Well, he must have kept busy pouring, that's all I can figure," snapped Maggie, "and the sooner you get it cleaned up the better."

Just then the bell at the door rang, signaling a new customer's arrival. Maggie pinched her lips tight shut and went to greet the two middle-aged women at the door.

"What on earth!" exclaimed one.

"We've had a minor accident," said Maggie grimly, "but we're cleaning it up *right now.*" She shot a meaningful look at Becca, who hurried toward the back room in search of the vacuum, trying not to crush any more Cheerios on her way. "Please come in and, uh, just watch your step."

"I don't know," the second woman said to her friend. "Sylvia said this was a nice, clean shop with good quality things, but I don't think so. Look at the floor. There is probably vermin in everything."

Becca smothered a laugh. She wasn't quite sure what vermin were—cockroaches, she thought, or maybe rats—but she knew she could crack Solana up with an imitation of these women.

"You just can't be too careful," one was saying to the other as they turned to leave. "My sister Nancy's girl got head lice from a secondhand hat once."

"Think it's funny, do you," Maggie challenged Becca, "losing customers and ruining the store's reputation?"

Becca sobered up. "I don't think they would have bought anything anyway, Maggie," she said. "It's not such a big deal," she added, looking at Alvaro, who was watching the confrontation wide-eyed and looked as if he were ready to cry. "He's only a little kid, and he didn't know any better."

"Maybe not, but *you* ought to know better. I trusted you, Becca. I left the store unattended to help you in the fitting room. You should never have left this—" Maggie looked angrily at Alvaro, "—this delinquent out here alone. For crying out loud, Becca, you're supposed to be helping the community center, not hurting it."

"Delinquent!" Becca's temper was rising to meet Maggie's. "So the kid spilled some Cheerios. It was an accident. Why are you so upset about it?"

Maggie looked at Becca. "Come here and tell me if this is an accident." She gestured to Alvaro. "Stand up." Clutching his Cheerios box tightly against his shirt, he awkwardly got up and stood, slightly hunched. "Give me the box," Maggie demanded.

"Maggie—" Becca began.

"Give me the box," Maggie repeated, pulling it out of Alvaro's grasp. He clutched at it, and as he did so a clatter of spoons fell from inside his shirt to the floor.

"Shoplifting," Maggie said.

• • •

Becca pushed aside the magazines scattered on the coffee table until she found the newsletter from the medical missions agency that was sponsoring Alvaro's treatment in the U.S. She flipped through the pages. *Before-and-after pictures. Endorsements. Children needing host families*. Aha! There it was. *Children awaiting adoption.*

She brought the newsletter to her room, locked her door, and sat down at her desk. She carefully read the page outlining the services provided by the agency. As she had thought, they not only placed kids like Alvaro in host homes during their medical treatment; the agency also handled international adoptions.

Next she turned to the section profiling children awaiting adoption. She read several profiles, then got out a pen and a notebook.

Alvaro is a six-year-old boy who recently recovered from severe burns. He speaks Spanish but is quickly learning English.

she wrote.

Becca examined the format of the adoption profiles in the newsletter. Health issues first, including any liabilities. Had she covered that? She read a few more samples, then added to her page.

He suffers some developmental delays but seems to be catching up fast.

She thought that was probably pretty accurate. Alvaro was little for his age—a runt, really—and he couldn't do a lot of things that American six-year-olds could do, like ride a two-wheeler or catch a baseball, but probably some of that was because he'd never had any practice before. She didn't think it was dishonest to say he was catching up fast.

What next? The profiles in the newsletter described some positive qualities. What could she list about Alvaro that would make someone want to adopt him? Becca leaned her mouth on her fist for a few moments, then went back to writing.

> Alvaro is determined and

she paused, looking for the right word—

> tenacious.

She thought about how he clung to her or her mom.

> He is affectionate and loyal.
> He loves speed.

She crossed that out.

> He seems to have a sense of adventure.

And he shoplifts, Becca thought. How do you describe that in an adoption ad? Finally she wrote,

> Alvaro would benefit from a loving family that can help him learn right from wrong.

Becca carefully recopied Alvaro's profile onto a clean page without any corrections or crossed-out lines. Not bad, she decided as she reread it. She felt pleased with herself for coming up with this solution.

The incident at the resale shop had made it all clear to her. She was feeling so good—about life, about Nate, even about Alvaro. But in just a few short minutes Alvaro had changed all that. Becca realized that he could never fit into their family. Like Maggie said, their family was the kind that made things better. Alvaro made things worse. It wasn't just that he was clingy and wet the bed. *Should I have put that in the profile?* she wondered. *No, probably not.* He was a shoplifter. Maybe he didn't understand exactly what he was doing, but that was all the more evidence that he just didn't fit in the McKinnon family. They were doers and givers. He was a taker.

Alvaro didn't belong in their family. But Becca didn't want to see him shipped off to an orphanage. The agency newsletter was the perfect solution. They could run Alvaro's profile and he'd probably get adopted by some nice Christian family that wasn't deeply involved in the kinds of service Becca's family was. Everybody would win.

The only thing left was to convince her parents.

The more she thought about it, the less Becca liked the idea of telling her parents about her idea. She hoped they'd see it was the best thing for everyone, but she knew that at first they'd be hurt and disappointed—probably with her. She decided the best plan of action was to leave them a note and let them get used to the idea on their own.

Tearing another sheet of paper out of her notebook, she wrote,

Dear mom and dad,

I saw this adoption placement newsletter and thought it might be a good solution for Alvaro. I wrote up a profile for him that we could submit. Think about it, will you?

Love,

Becca

She put the note, the profile, and the agency newsletter on her parents' bed. She threw away her first draft of the profile, then decided she didn't want anyone noticing it in the trash before her parents read her note, so she jammed it in her pocket. Looking at the clock, she realized it was bedtime. She got ready for bed and turned out the light, feeling a weird sense of anticipation and apprehension. Tomorrow would be a new day. Maybe the first day of getting back to normal.

chapter 12

"We read your note last night, Becca," her dad said at breakfast the next morning. "We talked about it a lot."

Becca glanced at her mother. From the look of it, they had talked about it all night. Her mother looked terrible—pale, with dark circles under reddened eyes. Becca suspected she'd been crying. A mental picture of her mother on the trail, looking young and happy, flashed through her mind. This morning her mom looked old and tired.

Becca licked her lips, which felt suddenly dry. She couldn't think of anything to say, so she didn't say anything.

"I guess you feel strongly that Alvaro doesn't belong in our family," her dad continued. Put that way, it sounded kind of harsh, but Becca had to agree. She did feel like that.

"He's a shoplifter, Dad. If you had been there to see Maggie's face when Alvaro dropped all those spoons . . ."

"If I had been there, Maggie might have used better judgment in handling the situation!" Becca's father said sharply.

"You can't say it's Maggie's fault," Becca protested.

"No, I'm not saying it's Maggie's fault. I'm not saying it's your fault either, Becca, but you should have kept a closer eye on Alvaro."

Becca looked down at her cereal bowl. She knew her dad was right. But that was part of the whole problem. Alvaro needed somebody to watch him all the time. How could they ever have a normal life with him in the family?

"You know that your mother and I would like to adopt Alvaro."

Becca nodded.

"And we know that you do not want us to adopt Alvaro."

Becca nodded again. "We've talked about this, Dad," she said. "You understand, don't you?"

Her dad said slowly, "I've heard your reasons, and I think I do understand, even though I don't feel the same way about it. I just wanted to ask one more time, because your mom and I will have to make a decision soon. It isn't fair to Alvaro to keep him hanging."

"I know, Dad," Becca answered. Her dad always tried to be fair. She hoped he'd remember to be fair to her too, not just to Alvaro.

• • •

After school Becca didn't feel much like going home—especially if her mother might still be crying. So she decided to bike over to the community center instead. She called home so her mom wouldn't worry, but she was secretly relieved to get the answering machine instead of her mother. Becca knew she was doing the right thing about Alvaro, but it wasn't very easy to face her parents just now.

The center was buzzing with activity when Becca arrived. "Hi, Becca!" the receptionist waved from her desk in the lobby. "Are you working or shopping today?"

"Working," Becca said. She realized she didn't want to face Maggie in the resale shop any more than she wanted to face her parents.

"Your friend Hannah's already here," the receptionist told her.

Great. One more person to avoid. Am I going to spend all day dodging people I don't want to see? Becca wondered.

"Becca! I didn't know you were coming today!" Mrs. Robeson checked her ever-present clipboard. "I'm shorthanded in the third- and fourth-grade room for the after-school program. Can you help?"

"Sure, Mrs. R. Wherever you need me," Becca answered as Mrs. Robeson steered her down the hall.

"Where's Alvaro today?" Mrs. Robeson asked.

"Oh, he's at home."

"Well, remember that you can always bring him along if you need to. He might benefit from being around children his age who speak English." Mrs. Robeson opened the door to the multiclassroom space segmented by portable dividers and ushered Becca inside.

Becca took a deep breath. "Actually, I'm not sure how much Alvaro will be coming to the center anymore. His treatment stay is about over," she said.

"Yes, but I thought his father had released him for adoption," Mrs. Robeson replied.

"He did," Becca said. "Alvaro's available for adoption now." There. She'd said it. "But that doesn't necessarily mean my family will be the ones to adopt him."

"Indeed?" Mrs. Robeson's eyebrows rose. "I hadn't realized." Looking over Becca's shoulder, she nodded and said briskly, "Hannah, Becca will be working with you today."

Great. Just great, Becca thought. *I wonder how much Hannah heard about Alvaro. Not that it matters. People are going to have to hear sometime.*

Turning, she looked Hannah coolly in the eye.

Hannah returned Becca's gaze, smiled, and said, "Hello, Becca. What a surprise seeing you here today."

"I do work here, too, you know," Becca said.

"Of course you do. But don't you usually only volunteer on Saturdays?"

"No," Becca said, biting her tongue. "Weekdays too. Just not lately."

"Oh," Hannah said. She looked about the room as she spoke. "I'm glad you're here. I can use the help. The children are doing homework right now. You can circulate and help them if they need it. When they've done all their school assignments they can take something from the enrichment box."

"I know the routine, Hannah," Becca replied. "I've been involved with the after-school program long before you ever moved to Copper Ridge." To prove her point, she walked swiftly to the enrichment box and picked it up just as Hannah was reaching for it. "I'll hand these activities out," she told Hannah. "I know which ones are the most popular."

"Hannah," called a little boy, waving his hand in the air, "I'm stuck on this math problem."

"I can help you," Becca said before Hannah had a chance to respond.

Over the next half hour, Becca made certain she was quicker on her feet and got to kids as soon as they raised their hands for help. It irked her that Hannah knew all their names and spent time talking quietly after Becca moved on to the next person.

At 4:30, Hannah said, "Story time," and went to the bookcase to select a book. By the time she had one off the shelf, Becca was already seated in the beanbag chair with the kids around her, leading a rousing rendition of "Going on a Bear Hunt."

"Oh, sorry, Hannah," she said sweetly when it was over. "Did you want to use this chair?"

Hannah didn't bite at the sarcasm. She simply smiled and said, "Only if you're through, Becca."

By six o'clock most of the children had been picked up by their parents and the remaining students went to the gym for free play. Becca and Hannah tidied up the area in silence.

"Becca, do you have a minute before you go?" Mrs. Robeson called from the hall. "Right now, if possible?"

"Sure, Mrs. R.," Becca answered.

Mrs. Robeson led Becca to her office and shut the door. Sitting behind her desk, she folded her hands and looked silently at Becca for a moment. Becca shifted in her chair; she was starting to feel a little like a kid in the principal's office.

"How would you evaluate what went on in the third- and fourth-grade room today?" Mrs. Robeson asked finally.

Becca was startled. Whatever she had expected, it wasn't this. Was Mrs. R. asking for her evaluation of Hannah? "Well, all the kids got their schoolwork done, and most of them had some time for enrichment. I think I got to work one-on-one with every child at least once."

"And what about Hannah?" Mrs. Robeson prompted. "What were her opportunities to interact with the children?"

"Well, Hannah's not that quick, so I guess she really didn't have all that much to contribute." Becca shifted uneasily in the chair.

Mrs. Robeson looked steadily at Becca, and Becca dropped her gaze.

"I disagree, Becca," Mrs. Robeson said finally. "I think Hannah has very much to offer. I have observed her serving breakfast, in the Reach Up room, and in the after-school program, and I am struck by how people are drawn to her."

"That's just her looks!" Becca said. "Every guy seems to go crazy over Hannah because she looks like some model. But that's all it is."

"No," said Mrs. Robeson, "it's not just her looks, and it's not just the men. I have watched her with the old ladies and with the little children. Hannah has a sweetness and a quiet spirit that people respond to." She looked severely at Becca. "You, however, seem to respond to it in a negative way. You may think nobody saw the little games you were playing today, but I did, and I won't stand for it, Becca. We do not have room for that kind of mean-spiritedness here."

If Mrs. Robeson had slapped her, Becca couldn't have felt more hurt. Tears pricked her eyes as she tried to think of a response.

Mrs. Robeson spoke more gently. "Becca, you know the biblical story of Mary and Martha, don't you?"

Unwilling to trust her voice, Becca nodded.

"I see you as a Martha, working at full speed in the kitchen. Hannah is more like Mary, sitting quietly at Jesus' feet."

"I'm not at all like Martha," Becca protested, finding her voice. "If anyone is the kind to be in the kitchen, that's Hannah." She thought of the Betty Crocker Club. "Hannah is the one who gets into folding napkins and . . ." she trailed off, not sure any longer what point she was trying to make.

"What makes a Martha is not the kitchen, but the *doing*," Mrs. Robeson said. "Like Martha, you're busy doing, doing, doing. And all the things you're doing are important things. They're good things. But when you see Hannah sitting at Jesus' feet—" Becca thought of Hannah sitting on the floor with the children while Becca hogged the beanbag chair. If lepers' feet were Jesus' feet to Mother Teresa, she supposed little children's feet could be Jesus' feet to Hannah. "When you see Hannah sitting at Jesus' feet," Mrs. Robeson continued, "you act just like Martha, and you want Hannah to be sent away." She added quietly, "But Jesus said Mary made the wiser choice. Being devoted to Jesus is always the wisest choice."

"Mrs. Robeson," Becca's voice came out choked-sounding, "I *am* devoted to Jesus! I love Jesus!"

"I know you love Jesus, Becca." Mrs. Robeson pushed a tissue box closer to Becca. "I'm not saying you don't. What I *am* saying is that you value *doing*. But sometimes *being* is just as important. Hannah did just as much ministry today by simply being with those little children as you did by rushing to answer every question before she could."

Mrs. Robeson got to her feet, so Becca stood up, too. "And I am saying," Mrs. Robeson said clearly, "that we can *not* have conflict among our workers. Do not force me to choose between you and Hannah. I would hate to lose you as a volunteer. Is my meaning clear?"

chapter 

"Ticket, please," the gondola operator said in a bored voice.

Becca showed him her pass and heaved her heavy bag of paragliding gear into the rack on top of the gondola. She took a seat inside and pressed her face against the clouded Plexiglas window, peering up the mountain. Since she'd never flown on a Friday before, she wondered if she knew any of the paragliders in the air or on the slope.

The gondola lurched into motion, and Becca sat back on the bench. She closed her eyes and took deep breaths, trying to focus herself the way she did before a big game. Consciously, she pictured herself wrapping up all her troubles in a big garbage bag and leaving them at the bottom of the mountain. She pictured herself gliding up the lift above them.

Trouble number one was her confrontation with Mrs. Robeson on Wednesday at the center. She had biked home and gone straight to her room. She felt she should tell someone, but she was too ashamed to tell her mom. Or anyone else.

Finally she pulled out paper and pencil and sat down to write a letter to Susie, the editor of *Brio* magazine, asking for advice. Susie's column was the first place Becca turned whenever a new *Brio* issue came. Becca knew Susie through Tyler's mom and their photo shoots, but she was too embarrassed about her situation to call her. *I'll send an anonymous letter instead*, she decided.

Dear Susie:

Have you ever gone hiking on a moraine? It looks like a regular mountainside from a distance, but when you get close you see that it's really a big pile of rubble—rocks and stones left over from when the glaciers scraped out a path. You have to test every step, because sometimes all those stones under your feet start to roll, and when they go, you go too.

The stones start sliding right out from under your feet, and you start to slip, so you move your feet fast to get your balance, and that makes the stones move faster. Pretty soon it's almost like you're running on a treadmill, not getting anywhere but just trying to stay upright, while all the while the ground is sliding out from under you. And you know that soon you'll be sliding down the side of the mountain with it.

My whole life has turned into a moraine.

All the things I count on—my friends, my family, the community center where I volunteer—are sliding out from under me. I thought I could stop it, but now I think I'm making it worse.

Especially at the community center. That was the one place where everything was going right. I felt like I was really making a difference for God. And I felt like the people there respected me.

Now all that's changed. And I don't even know quite how it happened—except that it has to do with Hannah. Only, somehow, it seems like it's my fault.

I'm afraid it is.

Becca reread her letter, then shook her head. What could anyone write in response to a rambling letter like hers? "Dear Moraine-slider, your best bet is to hope Hannah gets buried in the avalanche you seem to be making"?

No, definitely not the kind of answer Susie would give.

In the end, she wadded the letter up and threw it away. Like she wished she could throw away her troubles now.

Trouble number two was the scene at breakfast this morning. More accurately, the non-scene. Becca thought it might be easier if her parents yelled or carried on when they were upset, but they were just very quiet and gentle with her.

"The agency called again yesterday, Becca," her dad said.

Becca nodded. They had talked about it at supper.

"They feel we need to make the decision to adopt or release Alvaro. They have prospective parents waiting for children, and they don't feel it's fair to Alvaro to let him grow to love our family if we are not going to adopt him."

Becca bit her lip but didn't say anything.

"Your mother and I have made our decision."

Becca held her breath. She honestly didn't know what her dad would say next.

"We've taken into account your feelings—"

Oh, no, Becca thought. *Here comes the "However" part.*

"—and decided to release our rights to adopt Alvaro. I'll call the agency today."

Thank You, Lord, breathed Becca. *I know I didn't dare ask You about this, but thank You!*

Then Becca looked at her mother.

The gondola gave another lurch and Becca squeezed her eyes tighter, willing the picture of her mother's grieving face to vanish from her memory. What upset her most was the way her mother said good-bye as Becca headed off to school. Becca expected her to be angry or distant, but instead she held Becca close in a hard, wordless hug. When she finally let go, Becca saw tears in her eyes.

The memory of those tears stayed with Becca all day. The student council always went all out for homecoming week with special events every day, but Becca had a hard time getting into it today. It didn't help that today was pajama day. She tried to laugh at Jacie's big pink bunny rabbit slippers and be properly sympathetic that Solana had to wear a lab coat borrowed from the science lab after the dean noticed her flimsy baby-doll pajamas, but when Nate turned up at her locker in oversized Superman pj's, complete with cape, she burst into tears.

"What's the matter?" asked Nate, alarmed. "Did I do something wrong?"

"I don't know what's wrong," Becca admitted, wiping her nose on Nate's cape before she realized what she was doing. "I'm sorry," she said. "I don't usually cry."

"Don't worry about it," Nate said, for once seeming to know exactly what to do with his hands. He cupped Becca's chin in his palms and gently wiped away her tears with his thumbs. Tyler came by right then and started to make some smart-alecky comment, but Nate cut him off, saying, "Can't you see this girl needs a hug?" Tyler thrust his teddy bear into Becca's arms and he and Nate wrapped her in a big embrace. It wasn't the kind to send tingles down her spine, like she usually thought of with Nate; it was just warm and brotherly, like being wrapped in a down sleeping bag on a cold night.

Together, they bundled her out to the quad to find the rest of their friends. Becca thought she heard Nate whisper to Tyler, "Do that Alyeria thing, will you? Do *something!* I can't stand to see her so sad."

In the quad, each class had a booth set up. Jacie was at the Junior class booth doing body art, and Hannah was taking pictures. Becca noticed that Hannah was wearing a long skirt and button-down blouse, as usual. Probably her parents didn't approve of wearing pajamas in public.

"Jacie's working on getting Hannah on the yearbook staff," Solana told Becca. "Good idea, don't you think? Give the girl something to do without us." Solana sat on a table and arranged her lab coat in a way that Becca was sure the dean did not have in mind.

Becca felt like she should be happy. Here were her friends, gathered around her—and there was Hannah, on her own for once. Today her parents would release Alvaro's name for adoption by another family. Then her life would be her own again.

Somehow, though, she didn't feel like joining in the party atmosphere at school. When the others made plans to help Jacie put the finishing touches on the Junior class window downtown, Becca heard herself saying, "Sorry, I can't come. I have other plans." As soon as she said it, she knew what she wanted to do. She wanted to paraglide. Suddenly the desire to be in the air, feeling the rush of the wind around her, was almost unbearable. After school she raced home, grabbed her gear, and headed for the Copper Ridge ski slope.

Clang. The gondola locked into place at the top of the lift and swung gently while the few passengers stepped out onto the platform. Becca dragged her gear off the top and headed over to the ridge.

Almost unconsciously she began to walk with a little bounce in her step. About a half dozen paragliders were on the ridge, and several more in the air. Becca tipped her head back to watch the big, banana-shaped chutes gliding above her. Someone on the ground was doing a headstand and scissoring his legs back and forth in what the pilots called a "thermal salute." Becca's pace quickened. This would be her first try under thermal conditions—the warm afternoon updrafts that let a pilot circle lazily overhead instead of simply gliding to the bottom of the mountain like an airborne skier.

"Yo—Otis," Becca called, waving to one of the guys spreading out his chute on the ground. Otis looked up, waved, and loped over to Becca.

"You going up in this, Kid?" he asked. At 16, Becca was the youngest pilot—most were in their twenties. Becca had asked Otis about the narrow age range once, and he'd shrugged and said most teenagers probably didn't have the money it took to get started and most people over 30 didn't have the knee joints it took to land. Becca never asked Otis how old he was, but she thought he was one of the older guys there. He sort of took her under his wing, warding off the guys who tried to make passes at Becca and helping her learn the sport.

At first Becca had to ask Otis to translate everything the other pilots said, almost as if they were speaking a foreign language. The paragliding gear could be called a wing or a glider or a chute. The person gliding was a pilot—which struck Becca as funny, since there was no motor, but Otis explained that piloting a wing demanded just as much concentration as piloting anything with a motor.

"I'm going to give it a try," she said. "Have you been up yet?"

"No, I just got here," he said. "I probably caught the gondola before yours. Are you sure you're ready for thermals?" he asked.

"No," Becca admitted. "But I've got to learn sometime." She looked up at the cumulus clouds overhead. "I've been watching the clouds for a month just aching to get up there. I finally got out last Saturday afternoon, and there were no thermals!"

Otis shook his head. "How many solo flights have you done?"

"About 25."

"Kid, you're crazy! Bowser over there," Otis pointed to the guy doing the thermal salutes, "has done 70 and he still can hardly handle a thermal."

"I can do it," Becca said stubbornly. "What's the worst that can happen?"

"You could crash into another pilot."

Becca looked up. "Doesn't look too crowded to me."

"You could get blown off course."

"Where's to blow to?" Becca said. "Look at those guys—they're staying right in one place."

"That's because they're experienced pilots, Kid. That's why they make it look so easy," Otis insisted.

"Yeah?" said Becca. "Well, tell me this: How many solo flights have *you* done?"

"Around 500," Otis said, and laughed as Becca's jaw dropped.

"Well," she said, "after today I'll be up to 26 easy flights and one thermal."

"You don't give up, do you, Kid?" Otis said. "Okay. If you're going to do it, let Papa Otis get you set up at least." He glanced at the clouds. "And we'd better do it now; those clouds look like they could get overdeveloped pretty fast."

"What's that mean?" Becca asked as she opened her pack and pulled protective overalls over her shorts.

"When they get too big, it means the updrafts are unpredictable. They can drop you, or they can send you 30 miles over the next ridge." He glared at Becca. "If you see all the other pilots heading down, you head down too, hear me?"

"Yes, sir," Becca said with pretend meekness.

"And if you do get blown off course, remember to fly IFR."

"IFR?" Becca echoed. She always strapped a variometer to her leg to tell her the time, her altitude, and the length of her flight, but she didn't know if it gave her an IFR reading.

"I Follow Roads," explained Otis. "Friend of mine forgot to follow the roads and ended up packing out 20 miles one time. And you don't want to be toting this 30-pound bag o' rags," he said, slapping Becca's pack.

Becca pulled her triple-chain dog tags to the outside of her overalls.

"Whatcha got there?" Otis said. "ID? That's a good idea."

Becca smiled. "Well, sort of ID. These remind me who I am."

Otis raised an eyebrow. "You have problems with amnesia?"

"Not as long as I'm wearing these," Becca said. "See—this one says 'No Fear!' "

"That sounds like you, all right," Otis agreed.

"Yeah, I hope so," Becca said. "I got it on a retreat with my youth group from church. We were studying the book of Joshua, and at the end my youth leaders hung this around my neck and told me, 'Be strong and courageous; do not be terrified . . . for the Lord your God will be with you wherever you go.' "

"You believe in God?" Otis asked.

"Yeah, I do," Becca said. "Do you?"

"Don't really think much about Him," Otis said. "I've got better things to do with my time."

"Well, He thinks about you," Becca said. "You'd think He might have better things to do with His time, but I guess He figures you're pretty important." She showed Otis another dog tag. "That's what this one reminds me about. I got it at the community center where I volunteer. Every kid in the programs gets one of these."

She held it out and Otis read aloud, "For God so loved Becca that He gave His only Son."

"I've got one more," she told him. "I got this one at camp." She held it out. " 'What's in a name? Christian: I represent Christ.' " She grinned at Otis. "See what I mean? That *really* reminds me who I am!"

"Well, I don't know about Christ, Kid, but you're all right. If He's like you, He's probably an okay dude," Otis said.

"Oh, man, Otis," Becca said, "if you like me, you'll *really* like Christ. He's everything I try to be, only a million times better."

"Yeah, well maybe you'll have to introduce us some time," Otis joked.

"I could do that, Otis," Becca told him seriously. "You just tell me when."

Otis shook his head. "Not today. Today we've got to introduce you to your first thermal." He pulled the wing out of the pack while Becca pulled on her fleece pullover, helmet, and gloves. Then he helped her strap the pack, with her reserve chute in it, to her back.

Together they unrolled the main wing, checking carefully to make sure none of the dozen or so cords was tangled. When Otis was satisfied, Becca hooked the wing to the sides of her pack with two big clips that held all the individual lines.

"Okay," said Otis, "you might hit some turbulence up there. If you do, your wing's going to collapse on you. Pump your brake line and it'll fill back up."

"Got it," said Becca. "Pump the brake line."

"But don't pump it too hard, because you know the brake toggle is how you steer, and you don't want to steer yourself off course," Otis warned. "Are you right-handed or left-handed?"

"Right-handed," she said after a second. "Why?"

"Then your right side is your strong side. If your wing collapses, pull with your left hand first. That way you won't overcompensate."

"Is that important?" Becca asked.

"Only if you don't want to blow right over Copper Ridge and into the national forest. They can arrest you for landing on federal land, you know."

"Thanks for that thought, Otis," Becca said.

"No problem. Now let's watch Bowser launch, and you'll see what not to do."

Becca laughed. "Why do you always pick on poor Bowser?"

"He has no shame," Otis answered. "But he should. Watch."

Bowser stood downhill from his chute. He turned to face uphill and jerked the cords to his wing. Like a kite, the wing rose into the air, and Bowser turned quickly to face downhill.

"Move, you idiot," Otis said under his breath. "No sense of timing," he said to Becca.

Finally Bowser took a step or two downhill, but by now his wing was ahead of him. Bowser was pulled off his feet, but he didn't have enough momentum to clear the ground, and he bumped his rear end several times on the rocky mountainside. Otis shook his head. Bowser stumbled to his feet, racing now to catch up to his wing, tripped, and then finally lifted all the way off the ground, banging his feet on the top of a small tree as he went by.

By now even Becca was laughing, even though she knew she was even less experienced than Bowser.

"That's why we call him Bowser," Otis said. "There probably isn't a tree here that he hasn't lifted his leg at."

"You don't cut him any slack, do you, Otis?"

"Nope," said Otis. "The man's got no humility. I've got no use for anybody who can't admit they're wrong once in a while."

"Well," said Becca, "I guess it's my turn to learn some humility." She walked downhill, away from her wing, until the cords were taut, then turned to face uphill. Excitement started to prickle her skin, and she felt extra alert. She adjusted the harness, double-checked the clips on the sides of the pack, then gave a sharp tug on the cords. Her wing rose a foot or two into the air as the individual air pockets began to fill. Then, suddenly, it crumpled into a heap.

"Don't worry, Kid," called Otis. "You'll get it next time." He joined Becca as she spread out the heap of fabric once more. "Nervous?" he asked.

"Pumped," Becca said. "But no fear."

She sprinted downhill until the cords were taut, turned, and took a deep breath. Then she gave a tug on the cords. This time her wing snapped up and filled with air. Quickly Becca spun around to face downhill, making sure not to tangle her cords as she turned. She began to lope downhill in long, easy strides. One, two, three—and suddenly her feet were off the ground and she was running in air.

chapter 14

“Wahoo!” Becca yelled, as she sailed over the ridge and caught the updraft. Suddenly she shot straight up with a speed that took her breath away. So *that* was a thermal! What a rush!

Becca looked up at her wing, 35 feet above her in the air. She could just read the brand name: Promise, with the *M* shaped like miniature twin mountain peaks. Past the wing, nothing but sky and clouds.

She looked down and gasped. None of her previous flights had prepared her for what she saw. On her other flights, with no thermals to lift her, she had started at the mountain peak and, after a little bit of ridge lift, glided down. Now she was above the peak. She checked her altitude—almost 1,000 feet above it. Which put her at nearly 5,000 dizzying feet above the valley.

“No fear!” she shouted, and leaned back into her harness. It was almost like sitting in a lawn chair—a very, very high lawn chair. She'd never before had such a sensation of being so exposed.

Becca put her feet on the foot bar and pushed gingerly. The bar changed the tilt of the wing, which in turn affected her speed. She experimented with steering and quickly learned that the updrafts were very localized. If she drifted out of the thermal area, she lost altitude rapidly, but with careful steering she could circle around and catch the updraft again. She knew that experienced pilots measured their ability partly by how long they could stay aloft.

Out of the corner of her eye she saw someone losing altitude and thought she recognized Bowser's distinctive red-and-white wing. She maneuvered herself into a position where she could watch him. Now he was cutting back toward the thermals, but he'd already lost too much altitude to clear the top of the ridge. *It must be Bowser,* Becca thought. *It looks like he's going to crash right into the side of the mountain.* At the last second, he turned and began gliding down for a landing. Bowser's thermal ride hadn't lasted very long.

Suddenly she felt herself losing altitude and quickly steered back into the thermal range. For a while she played along the edge of the thermal, rising and falling like a kid playing on the escalators in a department store. Once Otis glided into her field of vision and gave her a thumbs-up, but he didn't come within yelling distance. For a second, Becca thought about trying to play chicken, then realized that would be even more stupid in a paraglider than in a car. She noticed that the experienced pilots all kept a respectful distance from one another. She thought about the consequences of tangling a wing with a 5,000-foot drop below her and shuddered.

Another shudder shook Becca, and she looked up to see her wing collapsing above her. She watched, fascinated—it looked like a genie returning to its bottle. Then she realized the danger she was in. *Turbulence!* She thought. *Quick, pump the brake line!* She gave several rapid tugs as she felt herself going into a free fall.

"God," she said aloud, "I'm praying with my eyes open. I know You're with me, so I'm not afraid—much."

Again she pumped the brake line, her eyes anxiously on the crumpled wing above her. Slowly the wind began to fill it, until with a sudden burst her free fall reversed and she shot back up on the thermal.

And over the wrong side of the ridge.

"What happened?" she asked out loud. "I did just what Otis said. I pulled with my left . . . Oh." Becca looked at her hand, still tightly gripped on the brake toggle. Not her left hand, but her right hand.

Quickly, she tugged on the left toggle, hoping to correct her course. Her fast reflexes had gotten her out of tight spots before, but this didn't look like one of those times. She had glided out of the thermal updraft, and already she'd lost too much altitude to hope to get back to her side of the mountain. If she steered back now, she'd be in no better shape than Bowser. Worse—at least he was on the right side of the ridge. *I guess I'm learning humility, anyway*, she thought. *Otis will be pleased.* At the thought of Otis, she began to laugh. *I wonder what he thought when he saw me zoom over the ridge in the wrong direction.*

Laughing made her feel better, and she set her mind to figuring out what to do next.

IFR, she remembered. *I follow roads*. She might be lost, but at least she could do her best to keep from being lost in the middle of nowhere. She spotted a road along the base of the ridge and decided to follow it. Maybe she'd be lucky and find a pass she could glide through before she lost too much altitude.

Before she had time to get her hopes up, Becca realized that she wouldn't be crossing any passes except on foot. Without the thermal updraft, she was losing altitude rapidly. She started looking for a good place to land and settled for a strip of what looked to be pasture running alongside the road.

She landed with a thump on ground so uneven that she stumbled and fell to her knees. Unstrapping the harness, she set about the tedious process of rolling up her wing and stuffing it in the pack. She pulled off the heavy overalls; thanks to her warm-blooded body, she didn't need their warmth down at this elevation. She took off the pullover too, but tied it around her waist instead of tucking it in the pack. She might want it later, if she didn't reach civilization before dark. She found her water bottle in the pack, took a long swallow, then clipped it in its nylon carrier to her belt.

When all her gear was stowed, she hoisted the pack onto her back and trudged to the road. A barbed-wire fence separated the pasture from the road, so Becca removed the pack and heaved it over the fence. She stepped on the lowest wire, lifted the next one, and carefully squeezed between them. On the road, she picked up her pack again and began hiking toward home. Except of course that there was a mountain ridge between her and home.

After about an hour, Becca was getting discouraged. The pack wasn't designed for distance hiking, and Becca's shoulders were getting sore. Her stomach was growling, so she dug in the pockets of her cargo shorts in search of something to eat. She found a power bar and a folded piece of notebook paper. Shrugging off the pack, she sat on the side of the road and peeled open the wrapper of the power bar. She took a bite, then unfolded the notebook paper.

AVAILABLE FOR ADOPTION

ALVARO IS A SIX-YEAR-OLD BOY WHO RECENTLY RECOVERED FROM SEVERE BURNS. HE SPEAKS SPANISH BUT IS QUICKLY LEARNING ENGLISH.

HE SUFFERS SOME DEVELOPMENTAL DELAYS BUT SEEMS TO BE CATCHING UP FAST.

ALVARO IS DETERMINED AND TENACIOUS.

HE IS AFFECTIONATE AND LOYAL.

~~HE LOVES SPEED.~~

HE SEEMS TO HAVE A SENSE OF ADVENTURE.

ALVARO WOULD BENEFIT FROM A LOVING FAMILY THAT CAN HELP HIM LEARN RIGHT FROM WRONG.

Looking at her first draft for the adoption profile, Becca recalled her mother's strained face this morning. This time, instead of trying mentally to throw the memory in the trash, Becca leaned back against her pack, closed her eyes, and let the memories come.

Solana, challenging her in the lunchroom: *You ought to be more consistent. You get all worked up about social justice and caring for the poor, but only when you can keep it at arm's length and do it once a month.*

Jacie, on the phone: *Not everyone has a life like yours. Not every-*

one has plenty of money, the perfect family, and parents who give them lots of freedom. Some people have to live within restrictions and do the best they can. If you can't accept that . . .

Tyler: *We made a pact. To be friends forever. To want the best for each other. To encourage each other to grow in our relationships with God.*

What was the best for her? If she asked her friends, what would they say she needed to do with Alvaro to grow in her relationship with God? Suddenly Becca realized that she hadn't asked her friends what they thought about Alvaro's situation. In fact, she'd tried pretty hard not to hear what they might say.

She thought she knew what Solana would say. Solana had practically said it, but Becca hadn't wanted to hear it. If her friends were voting "for" or "against" Alvaro, Solana would cast her vote "for."

What about Jacie? Jacie had talked to her more about Hannah than about Alvaro. Except for when she elbowed Becca in the ribs as if to tell her to stop trying to keep her family and friends to herself and learn to share. Jacie was always an includer. Tally another vote for Alvaro.

Tyler? With a guilty feeling, Becca realized she'd hardly talked to Tyler at all lately. She was too busy making him the enemy for having a crush on Hannah and taking her side in the bathroom incident. Like that made any sense. Becca wouldn't blame him if he didn't want anything to do with her right now, but look at how caring he'd been today at school. Tyler would vote for whatever he thought was best for Becca.

So what *was* best for Becca? In her mind she saw another picture: Hannah, glowing in the sunlight, saying, "Oh, Becca, Alvaro is just like you, isn't he?"

Of course he wasn't. That was part of the problem. He didn't fit in Becca's family at all. That's why Becca had written his adoption profile.

She opened her eyes to read the profile again.

Determined and tenacious. Well, that was true of her. How many times in the last week alone had she heard, "You don't give up, do you?"

Affectionate and loyal. Becca thought of her family and her best friends. She wouldn't have any of these problems sharing her family and friends with Alvaro and Hannah if she didn't care so much about them.

Loves speed. No question.

Seems to have a sense of adventure. Totally—and it was a good thing, considering where she was now.

Would benefit from a loving family that can help him learn right from wrong. Well, sure; that's what her family was all about.

Becca sat straight up. Alvaro *was* a lot like her! She was ready to bump him out of the family circle because he made some mistakes—but look at her. She could be crowned the queen of mistakes. She remembered what Otis said: "I've got no use for anybody who can't admit they're wrong once in a while." Well, she made a mistake in choosing bathrooms in the restaurant. She'd made a mistake in treating Hannah so badly at the community center. And she was wrong big time up in the sky with controlling that wing. *Maybe I* could *put up with a few mistakes from Alvaro now and then.*

Becca jumped up. "Oh, no, God." She pulled her pack onto her back and strode along the road, praying out loud. "You're not going to catch me that easily. We've been through this before, and it's all settled. Alvaro's leaving."

She took a swig of water and kept walking, trying to think of anything but Alvaro. *Thermals—what a rush! It's a whole new way to experience speed.* She walked. *Alvaro loves speed. He's so funny in that Superman cape . . .*

She stopped, frustrated with herself *and* God. She started walking faster, as if that would help leave unwanted thoughts behind. *I don't want to think about Alvaro. I* won't *think about Alvaro. Instead, I'll think about . . . food! That energy bar didn't put a dent in my hunger. I knew I should have eaten more before I came. That bowl of Cheerios wasn't enough to keep me going for long. Alvaro is so cute clinging to the box as if it were a stuffed animal—*

She shook her head, but snapshots of Alvaro clutching soggy remains of a Cheerio box flashed through her thoughts.

Am I clutching to the way things used to be with my friends and my family in the same way? she wondered. *Am I howling over what I can't have?*

She grimaced. God was not going to let her think about anything but Alvaro until they got it all worked out. "Okay, God," she said reluctantly. "When I said we'd talked about Alvaro before, that wasn't really the truth. I guess the truth is I talked *at* You and didn't listen to what You wanted to say. But can You blame me? Praying is dangerous business."

She shifted the pack to try to find a more comfortable position.

"You're not going to catch me by my prayers. Because I know You—once I start praying You might just go and change *me*, instead of what's going on around me."

She tried to move God away from the subject of Alvaro by compiling a mental list of circumstances she would like Him to change. But something kept nudging her mind back to the little boy.

She looked up at the changing clouds as if looking for God's face. "I wish I could wrestle You like Jacob did. But wrestling with You is never fair. You always win. But if it *could* be more equal, I'd do it so we could be done with it. Fair and square, winner take all."

Suddenly she began to laugh.

"That's just what You did, isn't it? You wrestled me right out of the sky! And now You've got me where I have to pay attention to You. You've got me right where You want me."

Something tugged at her deep inside. *Where God wants me is on my knees,* she realized. *Not telling Him what I want, but listening to what He wants for me and for Alvaro.* She stood still. *Am I ready to risk that? What if I ask God what He wants and He doesn't answer?* After a moment she had a scarier thought. *What if He does?*

"Okay, God. You win. I'll listen."

She slung off her pack and sat by the side of the road. After a minute she shifted to her knees. *My mind's too loud, God. I can't hear You. All I hear is me.* She closed her eyes.

Be still and know that I am God. She knew that verse from Sunday school. Quietly she began to hum the song. *Be still.* Pictures of Mary, sitting still. *Be still.*

I hate to be still!

Be still.

Gradually Becca realized that her mind wasn't racing along on its own the way it usually did. She felt the kind of calmness she experienced walking in the woods sometimes.

"But God," she protested, "I didn't hear a voice." *But I know what He wants*, she admitted to herself. *I don't know how, but I know.*

She picked up her pack and started walking again. *Shoot, I guess I've always known.*

It was getting dark and the temperature dropped with the darkness. Becca stopped to put on the overalls and fleece. As she did, her dog tags jangled. She fingered the one quoting Joshua 1:9. *Do not be terrified* . . . She took a deep breath, shouldered the heavy pack, and moved forward.

She closed her eyes briefly to start a prayer, but nothing came. When she opened them, she saw headlights. She didn't like the idea of meeting a stranger in the dark, but she didn't like the idea of being out all night, either. Finally she decided to flag the car down, but she took off her pack so she could make a run for it if she had to.

As the headlights approached, Becca jumped up and down on the side of the road and waved. With the light in her eyes, she couldn't even make out the shape of the vehicle. It slowed, and she could tell it was a red Jeep Cherokee. Becca's heart began to pound. *Could it be? There's no way—*

The Jeep stopped and the driver rolled down the window.

"Hey, stranger, want a ride?"

"Dad!" Becca cried with a sob of relief. "How did you ever find me?" she asked as they manhandled her gear into the back.

"Your guardian angel called the community center."

"What?" Becca said.

"That's what the switchboard operator at the center said, anyway," her dad told her. "Someone called the center asking if a girl named Becca volunteered there. The operator said yes, and the caller asked her to tell Becca's family that Becca was probably on this road. When the operator asked how he knew, he said something about wings. So she put two and two together and figured it was your guardian angel."

"Otis!" Becca whispered to herself. "What an amazing thing to do!"

"How did he think to call the community center?" her dad asked.

"Well, that's amazing, too," Becca said. "I was showing him my dog tags today, and I told him I got one at the community center where I volunteer. He must have gone through the phone book."

"Why didn't he just call us?" her dad asked.

"That's what's so amazing, Dad. He never knew my name till today. All the pilots just call me Kid. But today Otis saw my name on my dog tag. Only my first name, though—that's why he couldn't call you."

"Wow!" her dad says. "Do you believe in coincidence?"

"No way!" said Becca.

"Me neither," said her dad. "Do you know, is this Otis a Christian?"

"Uh-uh." Becca shook her head. "But I'm hoping he'll get interested. Why?"

"Because he said something else that made the operator think he was your guardian angel."

"I can't imagine," said Becca. "What did he say?"

"He said not to worry about you, because God was with you."

"Ahhh." Becca put her arms behind her head and stretched her stiff shoulders. "He was right."

They rode in silence for a while, then Becca said, tentatively, "Dad?"

"Yes?"

"I've been thinking about Alvaro." Becca saw her dad take his eyes of the road to look at her, and she continued quickly. "It's not what you think. I'm not going to complain about him." She smiled at her dad. "I realized you and Mom are right. We ought to adopt him."

"Oh, Becca." Her dad looked at her and shook his head. Becca felt hurt and disappointed. She hadn't expected her dad to praise her, exactly, but she had hoped he might have something nice to say.

"Becca," he said again. "I don't know what to say. You know I called the agency today to give him up. The social worker already had a couple interested in adopting him, so she suggested he be placed there right away. And we agreed." He looked at Becca. "Alvaro's gone, Honey."

chapter 15

JOURNAL

saturday, october 20

Tonight is homecoming. It seems like such a joke. Two weeks ago, all I wanted was to go to homecoming with Nate and to see Alvaro move out. I got what I wanted, but now I'm miserable.

My mom is miserable, too. And it's all my fault. This would never have happened if I hadn't been so selfish.

I got what I wanted and now nobody's happy.

I don't even want to wear my homecoming dress tonight. All I can think of

IS HOW I TURNED AGAINST ALVARO THE DAY I BOUGHT IT.

I DON'T THINK I'LL EVER EAT CHEERIOS AGAIN.

Becca dropped her pen and pressed her fist hard against her mouth. After a couple of minutes, she stood up decisively and went in search of her father.

"Dad," she said, "we can't just give up. We have to get Alvaro back."

"I told you, Becca," he said patiently. "I called the agency and left a message as soon as we got home last night. The social worker called back this morning and said they can't return Alvaro to us. As his foster parents, we had the first chance to adopt him, but once we signed the papers concluding his foster care with us, we lost any claim to him."

"But it was just one day! He can't even be settled in with the new family yet," Becca protested. "Can't they see it would be best for him to come home right away?"

"They don't see it that way, Honey," her dad said gently. "To the agency, it looks as if we can't make up our minds. Friday we say we don't want him, Saturday we do—how are they to know what we'll say on Sunday? *We* know we won't change our minds again, but they don't know that."

"But *you* always wanted Alvaro!" Becca cried. "It was only me that didn't want him! If we explained, they'd see that you and Mom are wonderful parents."

Her dad pulled her to him in a hug. With her face muffled against his shirt, Becca said, "Can't they at least tell us where he is so we can see him?"

"They think it's best for Alvaro not to upset him that way," her dad said. "You can understand that."

"I don't see how this couple even heard about Alvaro," Becca protested. She thought guiltily about the adoption profile she had written, but she knew her parents had never sent it in. "The agency shouldn't even have told them about him."

"I think they heard about Alvaro from a girl in their church who spent some time with him at the community center. She was telling them what a tenacious child he was, and that he was up for adoption through the medical missions agency. Since they were already approved through the same agency, they called and asked about him."

Becca pulled back and looked up at her dad. "Did *she* say he was tenacious? How do you know this?"

"Well, I wondered, the same as you, why the agency had a couple specifically interested in Alvaro as soon as we gave them our answer. I knew they wouldn't include him in their listing until we relinquished our rights, so I asked. The social worker wouldn't tell me the name of the couple, but she did explain the circumstances."

"Thanks, Dad," Becca said. "I've gotta go now. Can I use the car?"

"Sure, I guess," her dad said, looking a little surprised. "Where are you going?"

"To see a friend. Sort of. A sort of friend." Becca waved and rushed away.

● ● ●

After she rang the doorbell, Becca wiped her palms on her shorts. She felt sweaty and cold at the same time. Why didn't anyone answer the door? Impatiently, Becca punched the doorbell again, just as the door opened. A tow-headed boy said politely, "May I help you?"

"Yes!" Becca practically shouted. "I need to see Hannah! I mean, may I please speak with Hannah?"

"Just a moment, please," the boy said, and closed the door. Becca, whose family had never left anyone, not even a salesperson, on the doorstep in her memory, didn't know what to think. Would he get Hannah, or was he just going to leave her standing there? Just when she had decided to ring the doorbell again, Hannah opened the door.

"Oh. Hello, Becca," she said, sounding surprised. "Would you like to come in?"

Becca remained rooted to the front porch. "Hannah, I need your help. I know I don't deserve it because I haven't been very nice to you, and I totally apologize for being so rude and selfish but I really need your help."

Becca looked anxiously at Hannah, who stood perfectly still for a moment, then said, "Excuse me?"

Becca took a deep breath, but Hannah put up a hand. "No—don't say it all again. Won't you please come in?"

Becca just stood there. "Oh, Hannah, just tell me the name of the people from your church who are adopting Alvaro."

Hannah's face lit up with a smile. "Are they? That's wonderful! It's the Tukkers. She teaches second grade in our Sunday school, and I'm her assistant. She's wonderful with children Alvaro's age." Hannah smiled at Becca as if Becca had just given her a birthday present.

"Do you know where they live?" Becca demanded.

"Of course," Hannah said.

"Let's go, then." Becca took Hannah by the arm to lead her to the car. But Hannah pulled out of her grasp.

"Becca, what's this all about?"

"Didn't I tell you?" Becca said in exasperation. "They want to adopt Alvaro. But it's all a mistake and I have to stop them."

Hannah looked at Becca for a moment. "Is this a joke?" she finally asked uncertainly.

"No! No! It's not a joke! There's nothing funny about it!" Becca heard the note of hysteria in her voice and forced herself to calm down. "Listen, Hannah, I need to get Alvaro, and I need you to show me where he is."

Hannah's expression softened. "Your family wants to adopt Alvaro?" she said.

"Yes," said Becca, relieved that something at least had finally gotten through. "They always have. You see, there's been a mistake and I have to clear it up."

"You need to come in, Becca," Hannah said. "I might be able to help you, but we need to talk about it first. Please come in."

Reluctantly, Becca allowed Hannah to draw her inside. The front door led directly to a living area, and the first thing Becca saw was a couch crowded with three kids of various sizes, all as blond as Hannah. A girl stood at the far end of the room, dressed in sort of Dutch girl costume.

"Come on, Hannah," the costumed girl said. "The show is about to begin!"

Hannah walked over to her and pulled the child to her in a gentle hug. "Let me introduce our guest first, okay? Becca, this is Rebekah." Hannah kissed Rebekah on the top of the head, then let her go.

"I'm nine," said Rebekah, "and I'm an actress. My play is just about to start."

"Be patient, Rebekah," Hannah chided gently. She moved along the couch, touching each child on the arm as she introduced Becca. "This is Eli." Eli pulled his thumb out of his mouth long enough to say, "Hi," then popped it back in. "This is Sarah Ruth." Sarah Ruth smiled shyly. "This is Daniel." Becca recognized the boy who had first opened the door.

"Is this all of you?" Becca asked.

"No. There's Micah, too. He's upstairs."

"He won't watch my play," Rebekah pouted.

"Micah is a freshman at Stony Brook High School," Hannah said as if that would explain everything. The information surprised Becca even more. *I've known Hannah for nearly two months. How come I never knew she had a brother in our school?* she wondered. *I guess I haven't shown much interest.*

"Would you like to be seated for the play?" Rebekah asked politely. "It's starting in just a few moments."

"Thank you," Becca told her, trying to be polite in return, "but I'm in kind of a hurry."

"I'm going to talk with Becca right now," Hannah told Rebekah. "You can start the show without me, or you can have an intermission."

"You don't have the intermission before the play even *starts*," Rebekah said in an offended tone.

"You can if you like," Hannah said. "I'll prepare refreshments."

"Refreshments! Okay!" said Rebekah and tore out of the room at a sprint, Daniel close on her heels.

Hannah led Becca to the kitchen, where Rebekah and Daniel

were already seated at a big oak table. Hannah uncovered a large tin on the blue-tiled counter and set it on the table. "Banana muffins," she said to Becca. "Would you like one?"

"No, thanks. Listen, Hannah, I—"

"Excuse me while I pour the juice," Hannah said. "Once all the kids are settled we can go to my room to talk." So Becca waited as Hannah filled four glasses. The two youngest children—twins, Becca guessed—clambered into booster seats.

At last Hannah finished in the kitchen and led Becca up the stairs to her room. "Where are your parents?" Becca asked curiously as they climbed the stairs.

"They went out for the afternoon. I think they took a drive to the falls," Hannah said.

"Do you always have to take care of all your brothers and sisters?" Becca asked.

"Oh, no!" Hannah answered. "But I like to do it once in a while so my mom and dad can have some time together. Mom homeschools Rebekah and Elijah, and of course the twins are always home, so I like to give her a chance to get out."

She settled herself on her neatly made bed and patted the quilt to invite Becca to sit beside her. "Now tell me," she said, "what's all this about Alvaro?"

Becca shook her head. "I don't get it, Hannah. Why are you all of a sudden so friendly to me?"

Hannah raised her eyebrows slightly. "You're my sister in Christ," she said, as if that explained everything.

"We're sisters in Christ, but all week you've been saying as little to me as possible. Tell me how that makes sense," Becca said.

"A soft answer turneth away wrath," Hannah quoted. "But it seems like no matter what I said to you, you acted mad at me. So

I decided it was better to say as little as possible."

"So why talk to me now?"

"I'm hoping for some clarification."

"About *what?*"

Hannah flushed. "About that mean trick you played. Not only was I completely mortified, it really hurt my feelings."

"For the millionth time, Hannah, it wasn't a trick. It was a *mistake*. I made a dumb, stupid mistake. And I'm more sorry than I can tell you." Becca stood up. "But it hurts *my* feelings that you don't believe me."

Hannah looked searchingly at Becca. "Maybe I haven't believed you because you've been kind of rude to me from almost the first day of school. I tried to just let it roll off my back. I tried to understand that it's always hard to let a new person into a group of friends. I really wasn't asking for much—just some good Christian kids to sit with and a little help getting started in the school."

Becca felt a pang of guilt.

Hannah took a breath and looked at Becca. "I wish you'd tell me why you hate me so much."

Becca sat down heavily. "I don't hate you, Hannah."

"Becca, please pay me the courtesy of speaking the truth."

"Hannah, I came here to talk about Alvaro," Becca said. "I need to find him and you're the only one who can help me. Can't we put our differences aside so we can get him back?"

"I don't think I can help you until we resolve the problems between us," Hannah said. "Christ wants no strife between believers."

Becca eyed her speculatively. In spite of her modest image, Hannah was no pushover. Becca suspected that she would hold out for what she thought was right, no matter how hard Becca tried to rush her.

"Okay," Becca finally said. "You're right. I'm not saying I hate you, but you do irritate me."

"Why?" said Hannah, with a hint of a tremor in her voice.

"I don't know, Hannah. I've been trying to figure that out myself. I guess it's because you're bossy. You're always telling people what to think and how to think, and you have this whole stock of Christian pat answers to prove that your way of thinking is right and everybody else is wrong."

"I see," said Hannah quietly. "Anything else?"

"Well, yeah. It seems like you always think *your* way is *God's* way."

Hannah opened her mouth, then shut it again.

"I'm not saying you don't do nice things for people," Becca explained. "Like with your brothers and sisters—it looks like you're really great with them. But with us, the people who are supposed to be your friends, you come across as a real manipulator." Becca realized she was getting worked up and speaking too harshly. *But she asked for the truth*, she thought. *If I've gone this far I may as well keep going.*

"Like Jacie's portrait of Damien. You entered that in the contest because *you* thought that was the best thing to do, even though Jacie didn't. And homecoming. You don't think it's right to go, so nobody ought to go."

Hannah bit her lip as if she were trying to decide whether to respond or not. Tentatively, she said, "I really thought it was God's will for Jacie to enter the contest. I just wanted to be part of making it happen." She took a deep breath. "I never thought that would seem . . . manipulative."

Becca shifted her weight on the bed. *I hope Hannah doesn't think I'm doing the same thing to get Alvaro back. I'm not.* No, this plan *must* be God's will. She simply had to convince Hannah to help her.

"Can you explain what happened at the community center?" Hannah asked softly.

"Yeah—the community center," Becca began. But she couldn't really think of anything Hannah had done at the community center except be sweeter than Becca. "Well, I guess what happened there had nothing to do with anything you did wrong. It was my problem." *And I got myself into trouble with Mrs. R. and tried to blame it on you.* Becca squirmed uncomfortably. This list of faults wasn't ending up where she thought it would.

"Anything else?" Hannah asked.

"No."

Hannah sat silently for a few moments. Then she turned to face Becca. "Thank you for being honest with me." She smiled softly. "I'm sorry for irritating you. And I'm really sorry for what I've done to hurt you and our friends. Will you forgive me?"

If I say this, I have to mean it, Becca told herself. *It can't just be some phony Christian talk. And it can't be a lie to get Hannah to help me find Alvaro.* She closed her eyes and suddenly remembered the feel of her dad's arms around her, her face pressed into his shirt. *I've hurt my parents a lot worse than Hannah hurt me,* she realized. *And they forgave me before I even asked. And most of the hurt Hannah has caused has really been hurt I've brought on myself.*

"Yes, I forgive you," she said quietly, "and I owe you an apology. I've been totally unfair to you. I haven't liked you very much, but that wasn't completely because of you. A lot of it was because of me. I was jealous of you for coming in and taking Tyler's and

Jacie's attention. I wouldn't blame *you* for hating *me*." She swallowed. "Will you forgive me?"

After a long pause, Hannah said, "Yes." Then, after another long pause, "Why don't we pray together?" She reached out and took Becca's hands in hers.

Hannah was silent so long that Becca had just decided to peek, when Hannah began to pray out loud.

"Father, I didn't know I was hurting my *Brio* sister. You know I need friends. Help us to get past these bad feelings so we can get along. And help us know what will be best for Alvaro and the McKinnons without being unfair to Mr. and Mrs. Tukker." After a couple of seconds she whispered, "Becca—it's your turn."

"Oh! Um, God, I know it's my own fault Alvaro's gone, and if I were You I probably wouldn't answer me, so I'm glad You're not me—" Becca took a deep breath and started over. "God, I'm Yours, body and soul. I learned that last night and that's the way it's going to stay. So I'm not trying to bargain. I'm just asking You to please let us adopt Alvaro for my mother's sake. And for Jesus' sake. Amen."

Hannah reached over to give Becca a warm hug, and Becca rather awkwardly responded.

"Okay, *Brio* sis!" Hannah said. "Let's make a plan!"

chapter 16

"Turn left here."

Becca hesitated and Hannah pointed. "That way. It's the third house on the ri—uh, on my side. This brown one here."

Becca pulled up in front of the Tukkers' house and switched off the ignition. Now that they were actually here, all her impatience was gone. Instead, she felt terribly apprehensive. What made her think anyone would listen to her?

"The social worker must already be here," Hannah said as she led the way to the side door. "That car in the driveway doesn't belong to the Tukkers."

Becca saw Alvaro's tricycle in the driveway and felt another pang of fear. What if their plan didn't work?

"No fear," she whispered to herself. "God is with me."

When Mrs. Tukker ushered them into the kitchen, Becca

looked around for Alvaro, but she didn't see him.

"This is my friend Becca, whom I told you about," Hannah was saying to Mrs. Tukker. "She'd like to talk with you and Mr. Tukker, and with the social worker, too, as we discussed on the phone."

Becca marveled at how poised and comfortable Hannah seemed with adults, when she was often so socially inept with her peers.

"They're in the living room," said Mrs. Tukker. "Right through here. But I have to warn you that the social worker is not happy about all this."

Becca sat down on the edge of the couch and nervously looked from one adult to another. Now that she was actually here, she couldn't think of anything to say.

Hannah sat next to her and gently squeezed her arm. "Just tell them what you told me," she encouraged.

So Becca poured out the whole story. She admitted her frustrations with Alvaro and explained that she was the reason her parents agreed to relinquish their right to adopt him. She described her prayer and reflection the day before and how she'd come to the conclusion that Alvaro needed to be part of their family. Finally, her voice cracking, she described her mother's grief over losing Alvaro.

"Mr. and Mrs. Tukker, I know it's a terrible thing to ask you to give Alvaro back to us. But we've had time to grow to love him. Think how hard it is for us to give him up. You've only known him one day."

Becca waited in silence for someone to respond.

"Maybe you don't realize," said Mr. Tukker finally said, "that we've been praying for a child for years."

"Six and a half years, last month," Mrs. Tukker amended. "When Hannah described Alvaro to us, we felt he was an answer to prayer. What you're asking us to do is harder than you know."

Becca's mouth dropped. She hadn't expected this.

"Let me show you something," Mr. Tukker said, motioning Becca to a corner of the room. "I made this toy box myself."

"It's huge," Becca said.

"Feel the finish," Mr. Tukker urged. "Nice and smooth so he won't get any slivers. Go ahead, open it."

Becca lifted the lid to see toys and games of all kinds. Teddy bears, toy trucks, dolls, balls—it was like a miniature toy store.

"I worked on that toy box every night for months when we first started trying for a child," Mr. Tukker said, "and every night when I packed away my tools, I said a prayer for the child God would send us."

"We have books, too," Mrs. Tukker said. She reached into the bookcase behind her chair and pulled out a volume. "*Goodnight Moon*. I'm almost ashamed to tell you how many times I've read this book in the empty nursery, just anticipating the day I'd read it to my own little child at bedtime." She pulled out another book. "*Green Eggs and Ham*. This one's great for learning to read. Good for learning English too."

Becca looked from Mrs. Tukker to her husband. She was totally unprepared for this. She didn't know what to say. "I had no idea," she finally forced out. "I'm sorry. I only knew that we've loved Alvaro for over three months. I didn't realize you were waiting to love him for six and a half years."

She pressed her fist to her mouth. It had seemed so clear before she came. The McKinnons knew Alvaro; the Tukkers didn't. Therefore the McKinnons would miss him while the Tukkers would not. Now she realized what a shallow understanding she had of the love adoptive parents carry for a child.

"For clarification," the social worker asked Mr. and Mrs. Tukker, "just why did you agree to this meeting if you had no intention of relinquishing your claim on Alvaro?"

Becca hadn't thought about that, but it was a good question.

"We have a lot of respect for Hannah," Mrs. Tukker explained. "Besides the fact that she was the one who told us about Alvaro in the first place. When she told us Becca's story, we felt we owed it to Becca to let her see for herself Alvaro's home and to hear our side of the story. And we wanted *you* here," she said to the social worker, "to protect the interests of all parties, but especially Alvaro."

Mr. Tukker turned to Becca. "You're a gutsy girl, coming over here like this, and we want you to have every chance you need to feel confident that Alvaro is in a good home."

"You realize that our agency had already as a matter of policy denied the McKinnons' request to meet you," the social worker said icily.

"Indeed we did," agreed Mr. Tukker. "We felt that in this case compassion took precedence over policy." He smiled amiably at the social worker.

I like Mr. Tukker, Becca decided. *I didn't think I would, but I like him*.

Suddenly it seemed important to Becca that the Tukkers know a little bit about her family. She wanted them to respect her parents the way she was growing to respect Mr. and Mrs. Tukker.

"Would you like to hear a little about Alvaro's time in foster care?" she asked.

"We want to know as much about him as we can, dear," Mrs.

Tukker said eagerly. "Tell us everything you can." The social worker sighed and looked pointedly at her watch, but Becca ignored her.

She told about the process of being a foster family, and how excited they were when they got word that they had been chosen for Alvaro. She described his arrival in the United States and his early stay in the hospital for treatment. She tried to recall as exactly as possible her mother's impressions of those days and nights that she spent at the hospital with Alvaro.

She told funny stories about Alvaro's Superman pajamas and his Cheerios, and stories of frustration over his bandages and bed-wetting. She even told about Alvaro's shoplifting and was glad to see that the Tukkers weren't shocked. When she finished, she realized she had tears running down her cheeks, and so did Mrs. Tukker, who came over to the couch to sit beside Becca. She picked up Becca's hand in both of hers.

"You really love that little boy, don't you?" she said.

"Yeah, I do," said Becca. "Too bad I didn't figure it out until it was too late."

"Well, Becca, we wanted you to come so you could hear our side of the story and see how much we're ready to love Alvaro," Mr. Tukker said. "But I didn't expect to be so moved by your side of the story."

"It reminds me of that story in the Bible about Solomon," Hannah said, "when he had to decide which mother should get the baby. Only this is harder because in the Bible there was a good mom and a bad mom, and here everyone is on the good side."

"Who do you think your mom is like in that story, Becca?" Mr. Tukker asked.

"Oh, the woman who loved her child enough to give him up

rather than see him hurt," Becca said at once. "She already did that. She gave Alvaro up so he could have a home where everyone wanted him instead of—" Becca bit her lip. "Instead of a home with a sister who didn't think she wanted him."

Mrs. Tukker gathered Becca up into a big hug and rocked her gently.

"Do you know who I identify with in the story, dear?" she asked her husband.

"I think so," he said quietly. "But tell us."

"I identify with the woman who wanted a child so desperately she was willing to take the child another woman loved. It's not a pleasant thought." She looked at her husband and he nodded.

"What would happen to our status with the adoption agency if we decided not to complete the paperwork on Alvaro's adoption?" Mr. Tukker asked the social worker. "Would we go to the bottom of the list?"

Becca lifted her head off Mrs. Tucker's shoulder. What did he mean?

"No, there would be no penalty," replied the social worker.

Mr. Tukker knelt on the floor by the couch and took his wife's hands in his. "Well?" was all he said, but Becca could tell the couple was communicating with much more than words.

"Oh, yes," Mrs. Tukker answered. She smiled at Becca, her eyes brimming with tears. "You've convinced us, dear," she said. "Alvaro's a sweet little boy and we could love him forever—but as you say, we've known him less than 24 hours." She shook her head. "When I think of what your poor mother must be going through, I just can't consider taking her little boy away from her."

Becca gave a sob of relief that came out something like a snort. Mrs. Tukker patted her hand. "You're a fine daughter, Becca. I hope to have a daughter as devoted as you some day."

The social worker stood, the clipboard on which she'd been taking notes in her hand. "You seem to forget that this is not a private arrangement. Alvaro's welfare is the responsibility of the agency."

Becca looked at her in alarm. "What do you mean?"

"You have convinced Mr. and Mrs. Tukker of your case, but I have a deeper responsibility."

"Excuse me," interrupted Mr. Tukker, "but weren't the McKinnons already approved for Alvaro's adoption? I understood that the agency had done all that work before they ever offered them the option of adopting."

"Certainly that's true," said the social worker. "And legally the paperwork is all valid. But I also have a responsibility to use my judgment in the best interests of the child. An unstable teenager in the home who swings between accepting and rejecting the child is not a positive factor."

Becca bit back her panic and tried to keep the frantic note out of her voice. "I'm not swinging back and forth," she insisted. "I didn't think adopting Alvaro was a good idea at first, but I changed my mind. I definitely would accept Alvaro in the family."

"If you changed your mind once, what's to keep you from changing your mind again tomorrow?" asked the social worker.

"But I won't!" cried Becca. "Please believe me! I've prayed about this—I never did that when I was against adopting Alvaro."

"Can't you call Becca's parents?" suggested Mrs. Tukker. "They can tell you whether Becca is sincere or not."

"Actually, Mr. McKinnon called us already to inform us of Becca's decision," admitted the social worker. "I don't doubt that the family as a whole now wants to adopt Alvaro. But I'm lacking any unbiased evidence that Becca won't swing in the other direction next week."

"What kind of evidence are you looking for?" Hannah asked the social worker calmly. "Would a character witness be enough to give this case credibility?"

"Yes," the social worker agreed, "a character witness would be sufficient. But," she said pointedly, "I'm afraid that one teenage girl vouching for another is not adequate."

"I wasn't thinking of myself," Hannah assured her. "I had in mind the director of the homeless shelter at the Outreach Community Center. Perhaps you know her—a Mrs. Robeson?"

No, Hannah! Not Mrs. R.! Becca tried desperately to signal Hannah, but Hannah wasn't looking. *Hannah doesn't know about my confrontation with Mrs. R.*, Becca realized despairingly.

"Certainly I know Mrs. Robeson," said the social worker. "We often see each other at professional meetings."

"She's at the center on Saturdays, isn't she, Becca?" Hannah asked. She turned to the social worker. "Why don't you call her now and ask her about Becca McKinnon."

Oh, no! thought Becca as the social worker followed Mrs. Tukker to the phone. *What will Mrs. R. say about me? Please, God*, she begged, *please don't let this fall through. I promise I'll try never to be mean-spirited again, if only You'll let us adopt Alvaro. I know I don't deserve it*, she prayed, *but You wouldn't let my faults ruin this for my parents or Alvaro, would You?*

She listened as the social worker punched in the telephone number. Maybe Mrs. R. wouldn't be there. Then she couldn't give Becca a bad recommendation. *But if I don't get any recommendation, we might not get Alvaro either.*

Hannah was saying something to Mr. Tukker about their kindness in relinquishing Alvaro. Becca knew she should be joining in with her thanks, but all she could do was strain to hear the conversation in the kitchen. Should she go into the kitchen so she could hear it better? *No, I can't bear to see that social worker's face when Mrs. R. tells her what she really thinks of me. Why, oh why did I give in to that petty revenge on Hannah? I'm paying for it a hundred times over now!*

"Yes, Becca McKinnon," she heard the social worker say. "Oh reeeeally . . . Indeed . . ."

Indeed what? What was Mrs. R. saying?

"Is that so . . . Well, that's pretty definitive, I'd say . . . No, I don't think I need any more information. Thank you. Good-bye."

Becca heard the click of the phone hanging up and sat frozen on the couch. The social worker walked into the living room and fixed Becca with her gaze.

"Mrs. Robeson gives you a glowing recommendation, Becca," she said. "She tells me that you have volunteered faithfully every month for three years. That's certainly evidence of your ability to keep a commitment. I'm perfectly satisfied."

Becca suddenly felt weak all over. *Thank You, God!*

The social worker looked at the scribbled notes on her clipboard and frowned slightly. "Mrs. Robeson asked me to give you a message, but I'm not sure I've got it right. Something about she's glad it seems you're getting out of the kitchen." She looked at Becca inquiringly.

Becca nodded. "That's right." She thought about her times in meditation and prayer in the last two days. "Next time I see her I'll tell her she's right."

"Well, then," the social worker said briskly, "there's only one more person to consult."

Becca's smile faded. Would they never be finished?

The social worker went to the foot of the stairs and called. "Alvaro! Would you come down, please?"

Becca heard hesitant footsteps on the stairs, then saw Alvaro's face peering over the banister. "Becca!" he cried, and ran to grab her shirttail. Becca bent down to hug him, her dog tags clanking.

"That explains something I wondered about," exclaimed Mrs. Tukker, looking at Becca's dog tags. "We opened a new box of Cheerios this morning—" Becca and Hannah exchanged smiles "—and Alvaro found a dog tag necklace inside with a picture of some race car driver on it. He put it on right away and kept saying, '*Mi hermana, mi hermana.*' "

She reached out to show the girls Alvaro's dog tag. "I don't know any Spanish. What does *mi hermana* mean?"

Becca smiled. "My sister," she said.

chapter 17

Becca started honking the horn a block from home. By the time she pulled into the driveway, half the neighborhood was looking out their windows.

Her mom hurried out the door. “Becca, where have you—”

“Ta-da!” Becca interrupted with a flourish, lifting Alvaro from the car and putting him into her mother’s outstretched arms.

“Alvaro!” Mrs. McKinnon dropped to her knees and covered his little face with kisses. “Becca!” She cried tears of joy, randomly kissing parts of Becca’s head. “Tom! Tom! Come here!” she called.

Becca’s dad strode out of the house. He stopped when he saw Alvaro in Mrs. McKinnon’s arms, then bounded over to sweep Alvaro, Becca, and her mom into a giant bear hug. Just when Becca thought she was out of breath, he let go.

"What happened?" he demanded. "You didn't kidnap him, did you?"

"No!" Becca laughed, and told them the whole story, while they stood hugging in the driveway. When Becca had told every detail to her parents' satisfaction and had given them the temporary paperwork Mr. Tukker persuaded the social worker to draw up, they finally realized they should go inside.

"Oh!" exclaimed Becca's mom. "I completely forgot!"

"Forgot what?" Becca asked, too happy to care.

"Him," said her mother, pointing to a figure in the family room.

"Yo, Becca," Nate said. "Nice air hockey table you've got here." He looked at Becca's shorts and sandals, then down at his own crisp suit, and said, "I think I overdressed."

"Homecoming!" Becca said, with her hand to her mouth.

"Sure looks like it," Nate agreed, touching Alvaro lightly on the tip of his nose. "Welcome home, Superman."

"Nate, I'm so sorry! What time is it? I completely lost track," Becca said.

"I wondered about that," Nate said pleasantly. "When you said to come early to meet your parents, I sort of thought you'd be here, too. But that's okay. Your mom showed me all the pictures of you from when you were fat and funny-looking."

"Mother!" Becca said, in horror.

"He's making it up, Becca," her mother said calmly. "You were never fat. Just funny-looking."

"I'm going to go change," Becca said with dignity.

"Okay," said Nate. "Shall I go out and entertain whoever that is in the backseat of your car?"

Becca rushed to the window. "Hannah!" she said. "I was so

eager to get Alvaro home that I forgot to drop off Hannah! I can't believe she didn't say anything." She stopped. "Actually, I can believe it."

"We can drop her off on our way," suggested Nate. "Unless—do you still want to go out, or do you want to be home with your family tonight? Your parents told me all about Alvaro while you were gone," he explained.

Becca looked from her mom to her dad.

"Why don't you go out, Honey?" her mom said. "We'll have plenty of nights for family dinners with Alvaro now, thanks to you. Besides," she added in an undertone as Nate sauntered out to tell Hannah their plan, "that young man has very attractive dimples."

"Mother!" Becca drew herself up in mock horror. "Please! It's character that counts."

When she came downstairs in her Honduras blue dress, Nate gave a low whistle of appreciation. "Worth the wait," he said, and gave Becca his arm.

After a flurry of pictures, Nate helped Hannah into the back of his dad's classic '57 Chevy convertible. He turned to help Becca into the front when Tyler's beat-up Escort squealed into the driveway and screeched to a halt.

"We came as soon as we heard, Becca," Tyler said, lunging out of the car. "Or anyway, as soon as we found Solana."

Solana slithered out of the backseat, followed by Derek Harris, who looked as if nobody had told him what was going on yet. Jacie got out of the front passenger's seat and put her arms around Becca.

"Heard what?" Becca asked. Derek looked around as if he were as eager to hear the answer as she was.

"About Alvaro," Jacie said gently. "I called this afternoon to see if you wanted me to do your hair for homecoming, and your mom told me about Alvaro's placement and how upset you all were. We're so, so sorry, Becca."

"Becca doesn't look too upset," Solana commented.

"I'm not," said Becca buoyantly. "Everything worked out just perfectly. Alvaro's back, and he's ours for good." She beamed at her friends. "But it was amazing of you guys to come over." Derek seemed amazed, too.

"Tyler wanted to stop and get Hannah," Jacie whispered, "but I wasn't sure you'd want her here, so I talked him out of it."

"Oh, Hannah's here already," Becca said, opening Nate's car door and pulling Hannah to her feet. "She's the one who made it all happen." Becca smiled at Hannah, and Hannah looked modestly at her feet.

Under her breath Solana hummed the theme song from *The Twilight Zone*. "This is just getting too weird," she said. "I have to have the whole story."

"It's a long one," Becca warned.

"Tell you what," Nate said. "Becca and I were just getting ready to go out for dinner. How 'bout if we all go, and Becca can tell the story then?"

"We'll go," said Solana. Becca looked at Derek and bit back a laugh. He clearly had no idea how he had lost control of his date so completely.

"Where are you going?" Tyler asked.

"I've got reservations for the Copper Mining Company," Nate said. "They could probably make room for all of us if that sounds good to everybody."

"Oooh," sighed Jacie. "My favorite. But Hannah can't go—it isn't fair to leave Hannah."

"Yes, I can, Jacie," Hannah said. Everyone turned to stare at her. "While Becca was talking to the social worker, Mom called, wondering what was going on. Mrs. Tukker told her all about it. They were both so impressed with Becca, they agreed that I had chosen a great new friend." Hannah looked at Becca and gave her a conspiratorial smile.

Solana widened her eyes at Becca.

Hannah continued. "So I can go anywhere I want with you tonight, Becca. Well, except for the dance."

Okay, Becca thought, forcing herself to smile at Hannah. *Babysitting Hannah on my homecoming date was not quite how I had this evening planned. But things could be worse. After all, I'm the one who wanted a group date.*

"Well, let's go, then," she said aloud, her smile becoming genuine. "I'm starting to feel like I've spent half my life in this driveway already."

"I can't go like this!" Jacie said. "I'm not dressed for the Copper Mining Company."

"Solana and Becca are dressed enough for all of us," Tyler told her. "Make a statement."

After dinner they parked the other cars at the end of Main Street. Nate put the top down on the convertible and all seven of them piled in to cruise the downtown shop windows.

"It's like our own homecoming float," Jacie said as they perched on door frames and seatbacks, hanging half out of the car.

"There it is," shouted Solana. "There's Jacie's window! Nate, slow down so we can see it."

"I could put it in neutral if you like," said Nate, who was currently driving at five miles per hour.

"It's the same design as the fabric sculpture at the community center," Becca said, clapping her hands.

"But look who it is!" Solana exclaimed.

Nate parked the car in front of the window and they all piled out to identify the faces.

"That's you, Solana, near the top right."

"With thinner thighs. Thank you, Jacie!"

"Is that Tyler over there, or is that Malibu Ken?"

"Look! It's Hannah with Alvaro on her lap."

"Yeah, and he's holding onto Becca's shirt."

"Look, Tyler, it's your mom and dad."

There was a short silence, then Tyler said quietly, "Yeah, and look how happy they seem together."

"Who's the man with you, Jacie?" Nate asked.

"That's my dad," she said. "He lives in Sausalito."

"Jacie," said Solana, "who is that baby in my arms?"

Derek, looking startled, craned his neck for a better view.

"Who do you think it is?" Jacie answered.

"I think it's Alessandro," said Solana.

"Who?" said Derek.

"My baby brother that died."

Jacie smiled.

"What does it say across the corner?" asked Hannah. "I can't quite read it in the shadow."

Jacie quoted, " 'How good and pleasant to live together in unity.' Psalm 133:1."

As they walked back over to the car, Jacie murmured to Becca, "What are you going to do now? Drop Hannah off before you go to the dance?"

"I don't know," admitted Becca. "It seems kind of mean to just dump her. What do you think we should do?"

"You've got a great house for a party, Becca," Nate said, putting his head close to the whispering girls. "We could go there. You know," he winked, "play some air hockey. If Alvaro's still up, I'd love to take him for a ride in the convertible with his Superman cape."

"You don't want to miss the homecoming dance, though, do you?" Becca asked.

"It's okay by me," he said. "Everybody I want to see is right here." They stood smiling at each other until Tyler honked the horn.

"Yo! Driver! Can we have a little service please?"

Nate slid his long legs under the steering wheel, and Becca squeezed in between him and Hannah.

This doesn't make sense, she thought. *None of this is what I wanted. Alvaro's part of my family. Hannah's part of the* Brio *group. And it looks like we're skipping the homecoming dance to hang out at my house.*

So why am I so happy?

She took one last look at Jacie's window. *The more you have people who care about you, the more you can feel God's arms around you. And the more people you care for, the more you feel God's arms around you.*

"You did this, didn't You, God?" she whispered. "You did just what I was afraid You'd do. You listened to my prayers and You didn't change what's going on around me—You changed me." She leaned her head on Nate's shoulder and looked up into the sky. "Thanks, God," she whispered.

Then she turned to her friends in the backseat.

"Hey, anybody want to hang out at my house?"

Check Out Focus on the Family's

The Christy Miller Series

Teens across the country adore Christy Miller! She has a passion for life, but goes through a ton of heart-wrenching circumstances. Though the series takes you to a fictional world, it gives you plenty of "food for thought" on how to handle tough issues as they come up in your own life!

The Nikki Sheridan Series

An adventurous spirit leads Nikki Sheridan, an attractive high school junior, into events and situations that will sweep you into her world and leave you begging for the next book in this captivating, six-book set!

Sierra Jensen Series

The best-selling author of The Christy Miller Series leads you through the adventures of Sierra Jensen as she faces the same issues that you do as a teen today. You'll devour every exciting story, and she'll inspire you to examine your own life and make a deeper commitment to Christ!

Mind Over Media: The Power of Making Sound Entertainment Choices

You can't escape the ideas and images that come from the media, but you *can* weed through the bad and grasp the good! This video uses an exciting, MTV-style production to dissolve the misconceptions people have about the media. The companion book uses humor, questions, facts and stories to help you take charge of what enters your mind and then directs your actions.

Life on the Edge—Live!

This award-winning national radio call-in show gives teens like you something positive to tune in to every Saturday night. You'll get a chance to talk about the hottest issues of your generation—no topic is off-limits! See if it airs in your area by visiting us on the Web at www.lifeontheedgelive.com.